My Souls Desire

By

Londa B.

Enjoy
Thanks for your support!
Live life with much passion & purpose! God will get you there!
Be blessed
Londa B.

My Souls Desire by Yulonda Brown
Published by Aminia Books and Publishing

Cover Graphics and by Aminia Books and Publishing
Artwork: *HOT WOMAN*, by Darren W.

This book is a work of fiction. The events described here, are imaginary. The settings and characters are fictitious and do not represent specific places, living or dead people. Any resemblance is entirely coincidental.

ISBN- 10:0-9799154-7-3
IBSN-13: 978-0-9799154-7-5
Library of Congress Control Number: On File

Printed in the United States of America

FIRST PRINTING

~*Acknowledgements*~

I want to thank my Heavenly Father for bestowing this beautiful gift of writing upon me. Writing gives me a chance to release my spirit, comfort my soul while providing a chance to influence the masses. My ultimate goal is to motivate and inspire many people to change and grow. No change in life means you are living the same life…day after day, minus growth! You must understand that life is the procession to your funeral! Life as we know it will end for us all one day! Therefore, live, laugh and love hard! I hope that you will understand why I may call myself, The Writer with a Purpose. My dream is for people to become inspired and passionate in regards to living great lives while striving to make their dreams a reality. I implore you to… MAKE YOUR DREAMS COME TRUE!

Special thanks to loving family, including my husband Chad, and our beautiful children, Chanda, Marcia and Lil Chad. Thanks for understanding the hours at the computer and the many trips away from home. Thanks for tolerating me as well. I know I can be quite demanding at times! ;) I love you mom, dad and Cia-poo! Thanks to my entire family, you all have been supportive. I also want to show some love to my newfound family. I love you Aunt Cozetta, Uncle Billy, Uncle Willie and my cool ass cuz…Nat! Kiss them babies and slap the hubby! I must thank my business partner/ best friend and fellow author…O'Shea. Thanks for all the talks, the walks and great advice. To the brother that had all the answers for me, info searching, motivating, dream supporting brother, L.M. P. You have been wonderful. Life without you in this crazy lit world would have ended long time ago! MUAH! Thanks to Kulture First! I appreciate all your help and services. I would also like to thank my many special friends that have helped me in this crazy world. Thanks to: The Midwest Page Turners for all your support at local book signings. Thank you Niecy Davis, over at Foxy 95.5 Radio in St. Louis. Thanks girlfriend for all your love and support on and off the air! Thanks to Elaine and Cheryl over at Knowing Books and Café. You all showed me what I had before I realized it. Thank you! To my friends Ausar, Caswalyn, and Michael Harrison, love you all much! Thanks to my *"dream team,"* Debbie Tuckson, Naquisha and Kobe Seals, and all of my wonderful co-workers (especially my girl, Joyce Tesone! You sure know how to deal with a sista!) at St. Johns Med. Center. Last but not least, thanks to all of my friends and fellow writers on My Space and Writers Cafe. Your words of encouragement have been steady pillars placed at the foundation of my writing career. Thanks for your love, tolerance and support.

~Dedications~

I want to take this time to dedicate the book to everyone who has a dream. Dreams never come true if you never act upon what you have envisioned. Live your life for you. Your happiness and health depends upon it! The worst enemy a person can have is a lack of self-love for ones own being.

Mocha Latte, a local STL. Poet spoke truth into my heart and today it still beats strong to the rhythm of life. Her words were; "We all are stars; we just have to find where we shine the best." With that, I suggest you, follow your dreams and do what makes you extremely happy.

I want to thank a very special friend, Mr. C. Mohammed. You taught me the importance of letting go of things, which are dead! I am breathing so much better in this lifetime! God has truly introduced me to a lifetime friend! Thank you so much, my friend. Your courage, your loyalty and your trust is priceless! For those of you that struggle in your life, look to the Lord and let go! Whatever may be the source of your struggle, let go and let God! God is in control. What is for you will be, for no one can stop you from having what, "Thus said the Lord.

Foreword

Is Desirae Lewis a Stone cold freak, or a woman with an addiction to sex? That is what this book deals with. Yeah, it is erotic, neurotic and sometimes just damn NASTY! However, please watch for the key elements in this book. Many people day after day suffer with an addiction. The addiction can end in two ways. One, they admit they have a problem and seek help. Two, they DIE from their addiction. What do you consider an addiction? To me, anything that makes you lose focus of your values, your morals and causes you to display neurotic type behavior, is an addiction! My books will always have a purpose, because I write for the masses! My goal is to inspire and motivate you to think *and* live outside the box. *My Souls Desire* will definitely show you the way in which many live with an addiction. Life is no joke and death is calling names daily!

My

Souls

Desire

~Chapter 1~
The Reality of it All

Lying here with my legs spread wide, as my breast gravitate to their respective sides, I can feel my insides release a fluid of emptiness. This sight is fit for the eyes of a coroner only. Here I lay with life, but I feel as if I am dead! I try holding my breath on and off, hoping I would fade to black for a thousand days and nights. Facing the world was the last thing on my mind today! The way he forced himself on me was enough to make me want to blow my brains out! What would that accomplish? Not a damn thing! Hell, the definite splatter of matter, along with deep regret would be the only writings on the wall. I already knew leaving no explanation to my family, was not only selfish, but a one-way express ticket to hell. That is okay; I am not taking the punk way out. If he brought me to it...he will bring me through it! Lord, please show me the way!

After saying a quick prayer for strength, I rolled over and sat up on my side of the bed. I placed my head into the dry palms of my hands and the crying begins. I am going through the motion, but no tears flow. I am so dry from my eyes to my feet, that the only thing I can do is cry in a blistering pain. My soul is empty and it cries for relief.

"Lord, please deliver me from a life of nothing!" I begged the Lord and hoped that a sweet shower of forgiveness would fall upon me and induce a deep sleep. A sleep, which would help reveal all of my mistakes as well as provide me with a plan on how to live a fulfilled life. This way, I would awaken anew.

Much as my body cried for more rest, my mind was already running a mental marathon, and quickly approaching mile twenty! The day was saying my name like Destiny's Child sang. I love being the boss, but some days it is a true pain in the ass. Nonetheless, it is time to get moving. There was too much to do, and there were a few people that required 'letting go' of! I hate firing people, but sometimes folks can get a lil too damn comfortable on the job.

Before I could try to stand to my feet, depression saddled in and started to ride my back. No matter how much I twisted and turned my body, I could not shake *that* bitch off.

"Lord, this is too much to bear! Please Lord; tell me why I got married to Lance, so soon." I shamefully cried with my head now lowered between my thighs as if I were on an airplane embracing for impact. Rising to the voice of reason, it all came to me. I guess this is what I get for doing something without talking the Lord first! I knew my momma was not preaching just for the kick of shit! This is the drama, which unfolds like dirty laundry when you do not allow the Lord to order your steps. What did I *really* see in him?

I had to put the shit back onto myself! Hell, was there anyone else could I blame? I allowed it all to happen! No one can do shit to you and get away with it if you fight, block, defend and do whatever it takes by any means necessary. I let this shit happen for ten long assed years.

"He needs to go!" I yelled in a minute too late fury.

Today was the last time he climbed on top of me and performed and act lower than sex. He wasted himself inside of me too many times. This is no way for a woman to feel. My momma always said, "If sexual relations occur and there is no attachment, no feelings, no desire nor passion, then what the fuck are you fucking for?" That woman never told a lie. From her age, to if, it was her real hair or not…momma told the truth. All this time, the act of wasting on… and in one another has been occurring in my own damn marriage. Who can call this shit fulfilment? This isn't shit but roadside assistance!

Knocks at the door alert me as if the worst emergency ever was waiting to greet me, along with a team of cops. I hope it's not my husband, looking for sloppy seconds. For the gun I got sitting here...it may decide to shoot him instead of me!

"Hey, what are you doing here? How did you get through the gate?" I asked my over concerned friend, while trying to block the sun from my face.

"You need me here? I called your cell bout thirty times, why didn't you answer? *Mr. Nosy* asked in a suspect type of tone as he stuck his head in the door, investigating things for his own peace of mind.

"Look, I'm not in the mood to talk. It is over between Lance and me. I need his shit out today before three! I just need to find the storage where we can place his shit!"

"You finally ready to lose his ass huh?"

"Look, you've been here and you have helped so much, but I need to think out some things." I confessed while preparing to take my shower.

"Cook yourself something to eat and I'll be ready in a few. We can stop by my salon, check on a few thangs and then we can use the rest of the day to get his shit out!"

All I could care about right now was washing that asshole husband of mines out my hair, and off my body! Damn this shower feel so good right now. I tried to wash and scrub every part of my body. I did not want his essence to linger on me any longer. Hell, by the time, I am done with this shower; they might be calling me sugar cane, instead of brown sugar!

As I start to mentally rewind and process my thoughts about my current situation, a smile suddenly appears upon my face. “A true friend indeed is what that man is!” I chanted as I thought of the friendship my *so-called lover* and I have had for the last two years. He is a great listener and he has guided me and kept me motivated the whole way! “A friend indeed is what he is.” I chimed out once more. I have never been one to trust too many females! In addition, it seems that no other woman is really on my level. I have refused to allow women friends into my life. Finding a good girlfriend is like finding the perfect foundation! Now, that is some hard shit to do right there!

I can now see why momma never had too many women friends. I remember the first fight I had. I could hear momma yelling and cursing me to whip Sydney Michael’s ass. I knew I could not come home a loser, or momma would have killed me. After the fight, she asked me why we fought. I stood there looking silly and clueless as hell. Finally, I remembered and told her about the way Sydney was talking behind my back.

She simply stated before whipping my ass, "A bitch ain't shit, don't trust them! They lie, backstab and they come with bags of drama! You can't trust a bitch. Watch, one day ***life*** will ***show*** you exactly what I am saying." Then the whipping commenced from there. Was her point valid? Hell yeah it was! Until this day, I stay clear of women and all the drama they carry inside their expensive handbags and torn hearts. They present too many self-issues, especially the women that lack self-esteem and confidence. Those situations leave too much room for problems to develop with not only themselves, but for those that surround them as well.

As I stepped out of the shower, I heard a noise in my room. Grabbing my towel and my scissors, I came out ready to battle. The worst I feared was my husband coming home and attacking *my friend* in a mad rage. My husband was so sure that this *Buddy* of mines was my fuck friend! No matter what I said, he just knew we were fucking! Yet, he is still hanging around like the dead plants in our sunroom! I walked out and what I saw standing before me, was like no other exhibit I have seen in my lifetime!

"Let me show you what real love feels like girl!" my friend proclaimed, while he stood there in the birthday suit the Lord planned for him to wear thirty-five years ago! ***God is good…ALL THE TIME!***

Damn, this man was something more of a phenomenon! Six feet, five inches of black silk stood towering over my petite frame. His dick looked as if it was full of good, hard love! It was thick, and totally on point. Truly, I was really about to bow, for its presence captured every nerve in my body! It was quite a commanding piece! My pussy and my eyes started to twitch at the same time! No history of strokes in my family, so what in the hell is going on.

Heel girls, heel right now I say! This ain't the first time you two have been out the tent! Damn, my tits were swollen, full and leaking lust! I hoped that my face would not show any anticipation, or happiness for what stood before me. A sensuous throbbing pulsated between my thick thighs and my heart raced with fiery passion.

"*Buddy*, you're fucking a good friendship up! Please do not do this to us! You know too much, you my hang-ups, you know my weaknesses and you know what hurts!" I begged as I slowly backed up from destiny.

"Woman, don't start trippin. Come to me." he responded as he continued to walk towards me.

Next, he turned around, clicked the remote and I swore I felt as if I was front row, at a live Floetry concert. Floetry's song, *"Smile"* filled the room with a golden beam of love just as bright as the sun. *He knows I love me some Floetry! Talk about magic.* His dick rose even more, which only made me spread myself wide open, so he could see what my *sweet surrender* looked like.

He led me by my hand to the bed, treating me as if I was a Queen who had just stepped off her throne. From my crown to my toes, beauty beamed and glistened with the soul stirring sounds of Floetry, lightly echoing in the background. His touch was so gentle that it made me want it constantly, like my very own eyesight. The vision of this man on top of me, was so necessary.

"Stop, let me get rid of these sheets and let me...serve you correctly." he implored.

Now my nipples hardened and my thighs were clapping a name that was all too familiar, but this time it had a sense of importance as well as some clarity. I tightened my ponytail, because I feared this workout was going to be intense!

"Lay down." he requested, with a grin that was full of confidence! Damn, I loved it when a brother would smile like that before he bedded me. A smile like that meant his dick was the rocket that was going to land me right on another planet! A brother with confidence instilled not only his heart, but within his smile, is simply a divine sight. *Out of sight baby, take me there!*

"From the moment I laid eyes on you, you...became me! I felt your love, your sincerity, your honesty and I had to be with a woman like you. For years, you have cried into my ears, my face and even my heart. Today that crying stops. I want to introduce you to a new and joyous form of crying. The kind of crying that will have you bent over sick with love, for days! Let me love you the way you need loving. Close your eyes and lay back. You know its better sometimes when you lay back, close your eyes, while love slips deep inside!" this so called, friend of mines stated as he gently caressed my face, while stroking my body, and soul. Damn, a leaf ain't got a damn thing on me right now, I'm full of shakes and I am losing control; oh Lord, I'm falling.

"You making me shake baby! I can feel it! Is this what love feels like?" I whispered, as I looked upward to the ceiling with a blank stare, anticipating where he was going to lick next. He glided his paintbrush along the trim of my pussy. Damn the view from up north towards the south, gave me a new sense of direction. This man had me parted by the roots. His warm tongue instantly allowed me to release a heavy stream of liquid ecstasy, which only watered the tasteful buds of his tongue.

"Yes." He whispered back.

He looked up towards me to make sure his instant eye contacted only gave true definition to what he just spoke.

“Umph, Umph, Umph!” I moaned as he dived in. You would have thought I was lying on a sheet of ice, the way I twisted, wiggled and jerked in the bed. The entrance he made reminded me of a hot summer’s day at the pool. I loved the feeling of the sun-warmed water swallowing me whole, as I dive into the pool. I loved how the water rippled over my body and made me tingle all over, as I floated on top of the water.

His skills were record breaking, but there was no need to record this shit here. I knew this moment of pleasure would be an instant replay in my mind anytime. He glided that gold bar inside and out as if it was the recipe my insides craved. He slowly stirred me up, like no other. I could hear the union of our juices flowing and gushing right into one another. That sound alone raised me to another level. Sweating like crazy we both did what we could to hold onto one another without falling off. He pulled out from the love below and placed his face to the place once more. More toward the south was his favorite spot to be. I could tell by how *face deep,* he was! They say folks from the south make you feel at home. Well, his tongue did just that!

His tongue brushed the insides of me as if was the very brush that painted my room. The strokes of his tongue were long and very wide. It covered every angle of my pussy and had my clit swollen and anxious to release!

"Damn, ooh, please don't stop!" I cried.

"That crying sounds so much better to my ears!" he professed as he quickly snatched me back into his face. Damn his moans and the sound of pleasure on his behalf, made me even wetter. I love it when a brother shows how much he loves eating some black berry pie.

"Ooh, damn baby, please...please make it rain!" I begged while holding onto his ears. Hell, he seemed not to mind, because he was fiercely talking to my girl. The conversation between his tongue and my pussy was far better than any conversation I have indulged in. He was responding back to my pussy with every squeeze, every drip and every contraction. With each wiggle, and jiggle he licked back. *Damn....no need for anaesthetics, I am going under right now!*

"Yes!" I cried out. The rain clouds came, and the thunder rolled while this sister released a river. This feels like a puddle of ecstasy I am floating in with this man.

As I finished releasing myself, he proudly worked until silence occurred. Silence surrounded us and his hold gave me peace.

"See, I told you I would have you crying for a different reason. For years, you have cried to me and I have sat back, wanting, and waiting for this day to come. You are a real woman and you deserve a real man that can embrace you like the Golden Queen in which you are. I love you, Rae. When you get things right, I'll be here waiting to hold your hand. Not as a friend either!" he stated in a slowly but surely type of manner.

My eyes were finally ready to release those tears!

"Rae, Rae…woman wake up! You are running late!"

"Huh? What are you talking about…?" I slowed my speech and focused in on the ***real*** picture. I almost said the wrong damn name! I woke up in a total mess. My thighs were sweaty, my heart was still racing and my sheets were wet with the anticipation of seconds, from that heavenly dream I had just experienced.

Now I am all pissed off and back in the real world, so life moves on. I tended to my general wifely and mommy duties, and then finally, I tended to myself. Without even a bite to eat, I made my exit without one hello to the Mister.

~Chapter 2~

Dead and I Just Cannot Let Go!

"Why in the hell are you fucking storming out of here like this Rae?" Lance screamed as he walked heavily upon the heels of my favorite pair of Jimmy Choo's.

"Back up off me Lance!" I screamed. I halted my fury march and took a moment to look upwards. As the clouds glided by in the sky, hits and misses of raindrops trickled onto my face.

"This is going to be one awful day." I slowly whined as the sky began to roar and rumble back. Could this be a sign of release?

"Turn around and face me Desirae!"

"Lance, just stop with the bullshit, you seem to have your own ideas about how you want me to be! I'm my own woman with my own dreams and you seem not to give a damn about how I feel, so fuck you Lance!" I roared out as I extended my middle finger to give definition to what I had just stated.

Losing control in front of baby girl this morning was not what I wanted her to have for breakfast. I pray my baby can learn to understand what it means to stand up for self, no matter the circumstances. Women need to understand the importance of making our dreams a reality. Learning how to complete your goals on your timeline is a sermon I am always preaching. Those *'sideline'* days are so over for me! It is my time to shine. Running errands and coaching from the sidelines is outdated!

"Rae, stop and let's talk about this! You are over re-acting about this whole ordeal. You have been going to ***that*** doctor for months now and you seem to be getting worse. I have tried and so has your staff.

"What have you and my fucking staff done for me, Lance?" I questioned coming off my ***fuck you*** march to an about face, preparing to hear what the fuck he's talking about.

"Baby, you work way too much." Lance states while backing up from me, holding his hands outward trying to break my stride.

"Move out of my way Lance!" I demanded.

"You will listen up woman! Then you can leave!" Ray yelled as he held his arms out in front of me. Damn, he can look so good to me sometimes and other times I want to throw him out with the trash.

"Hurry up!" I demanded while brushing off my dress and re-affixing my hair. *Damn, I hope it does not start pouring down right now!*

"The late nights at the salon, the trips in and out of town and are too much to deal with! Even your employees feel that you have changed and your attitude is too much to bear!"

Okay, I am trying not to click at this point, but the tension is higher than any mountaintop I have ever climbed! Why do people lack the nerve to express themselves from the moment a problem occurs? I mean what is up with the wait and see shit? That method only gives the issue at hand time to ferment! Fermenting is good for beer, not relationships! What happens after shit has been simmering? A dramatic EXPLOSION occurs! Now that's what's up! You must tend to the shit when it surfaces!

Pointing my finger in the air as if I am firing off rounds, and yelling to the highest octave possible will really give our neighbors something to chat about this morning!

"You got me fucked up Lance, you *really* don't have a clue to what is going on, but I tell you what...you will by sunrise."

"Sunrise?" He questions as if he was offended while he takes a defensive stance. *I can't stand his ass. The site of him is making me sick!*

"Yes, with every new sunrise, there comes a fucking change and you'll see what that change will be."

Deeply staring into my husband's chestnut brown eyes, I rapidly inhale and exhale my frustration. Minute by minute I try to contain my anger by balling my fists as tight as I possibly can, but I can feel the anger leaking out the cracks of my fists. I feel Lance's sincerity to resolve our conflict, but I instantly snap out of my *"matters of the heart moment"* and reality sticks the hell out of me, like a thorn in my finger.

"Lance, what are your motives?" I asked while pressing on the gas trying my best to accelerate his answer, before speeding off.

"Listen baby," he responds in a hurried voice as he paces his self along the car, while I slowly lift my foot off the brake.

"I know we have an agreement not to discuss work at home or to even talk with each others work associates, but your people came to me. They were only concerned about you. Everyone knows that the ownership of these four-day spas and all your community work is taking you into overload. Please tell me you miss home, me, even our daughter. I thought this doctor you picked would help you in managing your stress, but he hasn't done shit!"

I feel so bad because I can see the pain in his facial expressions and I hear the anguish in his voice. My feelings for this marriage have exhausted like a marathon runner. The pain of living in a loveless and passionless marriage for the last ten years is enough for me to call it quits. I gave Lance's ass many chances and even suggested counselling, but he felt it was more of my problem than his own problem. I am tired and ready to move on.

"Lance, for years I've sat by and watched you work at becoming a very successful in the real estate biz. I have attended all the parties, helped you with community work and placed my own personal goals and dreams on hold until your shit went platinum! Now that my career is doing great and I'm well established; you suddenly want me to back down?" *This thought alone, send my eyeballs into a constant roll.*

"I'm not asking you to halt all of your activities," he grunts out while he avoids all possible eye contact.

"Then what is it that you want from me?" I asked while bobbing and weaving, trying to re-connect my eyes with his.

"I just want my wife home. I miss us spending time together, going places and being there as husband and wife at our daughters school events. Damn baby, I miss you and me, one on one girl!" *I need a face towel, because he is spitting bullshit all in my face!*

"Well okay, what happens at the end of the day? Shall I draw up yo bath water, tend to the fields, cleans yo house, then tend to making a good meal? Oh, yeah Ise can even fuck your brains out onto the pillow and have you in bed all cozy and snugly by ten if you like Bossa!" I yelled, as I mimicked a good old girl shuffle in the seat of my car.

"What's going to happen when the sun settles?" I asked, while jerking back and forth on the steering wheel as if I were suffering from fifth degree road rage.

"I'm tired, unfulfilled and I am looking for something that has nothing to do with my career. I WISH I *had* a real good reason to stay home these days but I don't."

"Not even for our daughter?" He questions as he reaches for my hand.

"You know Rachel has nothing to do with any of this." snatching my hand back from his hand back inside my car window.

"Don't ever fix your mouth to put Rachel in *our* problems, like it will change what is going on at this very moment. I love my child. I have done everything I can to provide for her mentally, physically and financially."

As I am going off, I notice that he is staring far beyond my face. He is probably reminiscing about some past time in our lives were we once were civil and respectable towards each another.

"What the hell are you laughing at? I know I didn't say a damn thing funny."

"You missed one."

"Missed what Lance?"

"What about Rachel's emotions Rae?"

"My baby is fine, we talk all the time and she hasn't said anything to me out of the ordinary. Are you just making this up as we argue along?"

"No, I'm not Rae! Maybe you don't know your child as good as you think you do!"

"Lance, you personally are aware of all the struggles my life has contained. I really have no respect for you in regards to how you are trying to interject our child into this situation." At this point, time is not on our side and I cannot help but to think about heading out of town this weekend for a little *me* time.

"Baby, I am not using Rachel for anything. I am simply trying to show you what you are missing. You have truly come along way. You have worked very hard at being the best at everything that you do. A self- made millionaire by your mid twenties, a lovely wife, a nurturing mother, and a very well respected community figure. Do you know how many people wish they could wear a pair of your shoes?"

Some people have all the nerve! My face had to look like I had just received about a million Botox injections. I was stiff with shock at what flew out of Lance's mouth.

"That's the problem Lance. Everyone should want to wear his or her own fucking shoes! I made what I had work for me, and people should try applying that formula to their own lives and face it!"

At this point, I am beyond listening to anything he has to say. I hear him, but I am not feeling it. My heart beats to a new rhythm. The increased amount of bullshit and lack of love for Lance caused this conversion. This shit goes much deeper than any river I have ever swum.

"Lance, we need to have this talk this evening. I have my doctor's appointment, clients at the salon will be waiting and I just need to leave before I show that *old* me!"

Looking disappointed and hurt all at the same time, he lifts up from the car window with a look of defeat.

"We'll finish this talk tonight!" I yelled

"Rae, wait you forgot...."

Not giving a damn about what he is trying to say, I sped off from the mansion in route to make it to my doctor's appointment.

"Call Denise" I shouted out to my intercom system.

"Calling Denise" the robotic operator responded.

"Rae-Rae? Bout time you checked in with your sis!"

"Hey what's up Niecy?" I grumbled, while using my phone smile, trying to disguise my anger.

"Oh shit!" she yelled.

"What, is it?" I asked, knowing she is about to bust me clean out.

"You and Lance had a fight, haven't you?"

Damn, once again- she figured me out! I can never hide shit from this girl.

"Yes, we did." I slowly replied.

Damn, I hate telling her some of my business at times! I just feel she is somewhere giving thanks to the good Lord, after we chat on the phone that she is not me! It is like; fuck the Young and the Restless when she has my crazy shit giving her life some spice and drama.

"You want to talk? I will listen for days on end. You know I don't have shit to do, until the kids come home."

"Look sis, I'll be over after I leave the salon tonight. I have a full day and I am already tired. Just to help you understand what your big sis is going through listen to this.

"Go head, I'm listening."

"You know how two people can lay in the same bed, but neither one of them is sleeping?"

"Damn Rae, that's bad."

"Hell, yeah it is. I may as well be lying beside a stranger. Listen, it's not that I fear lying next to him because of safety issues. I think it's the fact that I know this shit should have been over long time ago. I guess neither one of us, wants to be the first to say goodbye. Now, is that some cliché or Jackson 5 type shit to say, or what? I mean, in certain circumstances most people are up like that because they are mad at each other and no resolutions occurred before bedtime. In addition, you know they nasty asses are anticipating the make-up session that hangs around the corner of their sheets. In some cases, it could be that they are losing sleep because of the stresses concerning their bills.

Well you know money is not our problem, so now what?"

"Rae, what do you plan on doing?" Niecy quizzed, while she hungrily munched on some chips loud as hell in my ear.

"Damn, could you cut that fucking crunching out? You got me feeling like I'm ear deep in a bag of pork rinds myself!"

"Whoops! I know how much you hate that! Sorry sis." She apologized with her mouth still full.

"Anyway, I don't know what I'm going to do but I need some peace in my life. This shit is dead and someone has to let go!" I said while looking off into distant space.

"You're right! You have to apply this to real life occurrences. When a person dies, as sad as we are what do we do next?"

"Have a funeral." I hesitantly replied.

"Damn right we do! I know it is hard to accept the fact that your marriage is over, but it is time to call for a service, because the dead cannot come back! Let that shit go!"

Damn her words cut deep into my soul. The truth really hurts. She may as well be the older sister because her knowledge and her strength amaze me. I have never leaned on any body more since momma passed, other than my sister.

"You still mess..."

"Please don't ask me about him." I commanded as I placed my hand on my forehead while navigating my Benz down highway forty.

"He is not the reason why I want to leave Lance. My marriage to Lance was all about convenience. Lance had the money, the career, and the looks. Hell, we both made such a great power couple. Image was everything to me at that time. Now, all I want is to feel just as good as I look. I don't need you lecturing me either." I snapped while trying to figure out why this nosy assed chick is trying to read my lips at the stoplight.

"What!" I screamed while jumping at the chick in the car next to me through my car window. People can be so nosy, as if they do not have problems of their own to fix.

"Rae, who are you yelling at?"

"An asshole, that's what. She is estimating the hell out of me. Searching the inside of my mouth, like a dentist! I guess she is looking for cavities. Hope she finds a fucking cavity!"

"Okay, forget that asshole. Just promise me that you'll be careful and you will seek the Lord in all that you do."

"Okay, I will. Quit tripping girl."

"I'm not tripping Rae. You have to be careful on how you break this marriage apart. I mean, do you actually think Lance will throw this shit over his shoulder like a piece of trash, and move on with life? I mean you are too old and shit to be appearing on the back of a fucking milk carton. I mean, neither should the kids, but yo grown ass?" she uncontrollably giggled, while she was still munching on those damn chips.

"Ha, ha, very fucking funny! Just make sure his mug shot makes it to the post-office if some shit happens to me! You know you big time if your shit made it to the post-office. That's a red alert to the nation that your ass has really fucked up!" At this point, I am trying to keep my cool, by not crashing my car while laughing at her silly ass!

"Trust me when I say I'm always at the head of the line and not the back. Shit, why you think I'm always up at night?"

"One can assume that you're hunting for new dick in your life." Niecy teased.

"You're silly ass hell Niecy."

For a moment, there was a pause, because I know she was trying to press her ear up hard against the phone, as if she would be able to feel me.

"I love you sis." Niecy said.

"Love you too." I said while trying not to choke on my tears. I know that girl loves me hard. She is all I have in this world.

Lovely fall days like today allow me take the time to slow down and appreciate everything around me. With my windows lowered to the halfway point, my sexiness became visual to a certain degree of pleasure for the drivers that passed by. The fall breeze tunnels up my nostrils and refreshes my mind, as I listen to the smooth tunes of Will Downing. I play Brother Will when a chill down is in my forecast. If that does not happen, St. Louis may be experiencing a severe storm front! It will not take a damn meteorologist to tell nobody that shit either. All it takes is a few minutes of Will to sing some sensuous chords of sweet love, and I forget all my troubles. Well at least until they surface again.

Londa B.

I love how the city of St. Louis is changing its downtown area. It has that New York feel, only a lot smaller though. People from the Lou have no problem telling you to screw off, put you in your place, and go on with life; as if shit is all-good again. On the other side, there are plenty of sweet and down to earth people with good hearts, which give voice to their actions. That act alone is what gives true meaning to St. Louis being a "Show Me State."

Why do people continue to hold onto things, which have expired a long time ago? See, that is why carrying dead weight is such a damn burden.

~Chapter 3~

Good Doctor-Bad Doctor

I arrive to the doctor's office in good time and another sigh of relief escapes my body. This doctor may as well clear his schedule today, because I need to get some things off my chest today.
Just as I was about to shut my car door I noticed this parking attendant walking towards me with the looks of awe, and curiosity planted on his face. Oh, those damn teen-age years! Just when you think you all fly and shit, other people simply view you as a dumb looking kid. Thank God, those days are long over!

"Nice Benz, is it 05 or 06 model." He eagerly asks.
Does he know anything about cars?

"It's a 06 Benz SL Roadster... SL600, that is." I responded while wiping off some dust that was laying on my ride.

Why do I suddenly feel compelled to slap the hell out of this kid? I mean my hand is actually fucking twitching and jerking real bad! I know the doctor never told me I had carpal tunnel or reflex issues, so what the hell.

"Do I owe you a tip or some thing?" I asked while noticing that this kid is into everything else, ***BUT*** his damn job.
He heckles as if I insulted him, as he drives his eyeballs around the curves of my body. He finally decides to park his eyes on my juicy ass.

"No lady, you don't owe me a tip, I was just trying to see if you needed directions into the building and to tell you what a nice ride you got." He quickly responds as he shifts his attention chest level.

Yeah right, this joker is too busy looking at my 38 double D's!

"No sweetheart, I'm fine, and I'm well aware on how to get inside the building. If I get lost along the way I'm sure the signs posted on just about every wall in the building, will help me. Thanks but no thanks."

"Another rich, snot nosed bitch!" he mumbles as he walks away.

I continue go on without word. I simply do not feel like being on the news tonight for whipping some young punk's ass!

I figure I give myself a once over using my car window as a mirror, before I head in. Even though my mind seems fucked up at times...I can't look fucked up too. I got an image to protect. I can't help but smile (while glancing in the car window) because I get better and better with time. Hair is in place...check; nails looking well manicured...check, lips shining like liquid candy...check. I love the way this wrap dress is wrapping around all of my curves. Oh Lord, I better get going before I touch myself!

"Morning, Mrs. Lewis!" The door attendant yelps out like a puppy in love.

"Hello Mr. Thomas. How is door duty today?"

"Ah you know, a few tips here, no tips there. Same old shit! I can tell you something though." He confides, as he gets closer to me.

"What's that sweetie?" I asked while dusting his jacket off.

"When you walk your thick, fine self through that door, my day turns out to be a great one; no matter how many times people stiff me." He then belts out a thunderous laugh, which quickly ends with a round of coughs and gagging attacks!

"What does your old lady do with you Mr. Thomas?" I asked while patting him on his back to make sure he coughs up the rest of the bullshit that is in him.

"Nothing at all, baby!" he answers while doing some old ancient shuffle with his tongue hanging damn near down to the ground.

Is this old man trying to work me over or what?

"Tell the Mrs. to give me a call; I got a few stories to tell her."

"You know I'm jazzing you up Mrs. Lewis." He states in his professional tone of voice, while trying to act as if he was not just trying to hit on me a second ago.

"I know handsome" I smiled as I made my entrance onto the elevator. *Look at his ass. He can't help but to stare at me until the final closing of the doors.* These old men know they crack me up. Their old asses be on all types of meds and be sick as hell. Lord only knows why they like chasing young tail. I can't imagine meeting his kids at the funeral, hitting me up with all types of questions about he died. I'll tell their ass the same thing old girl in the Color Purple did when Celie went to her father's funeral and asked the young woman how their daddy died.

I think was her reply went something like, "On top of me."

From there, old Rae might be on the run because that shit that would clear a funeral clean out!

Damn, I can't help but to laugh all the way up on the elevator ride. If I passed, anyone waiting on an elevator down folks will probably think a lunatic is stuck inside the elevator; because of the way, I'm carrying on!

I can't help but to belt out another chorus of laughs before the doors open. Let me stop playing and adjust myself, before this doctor starts thinking that I have given up on being sane.

I opened the door to the suite and into the suite, and I am mesmerized with the style, upkeep, and the total office environment. I had to step back out of the door, just to make sure I had the right suite number.

"Six twenty six, yup it's the right one."

This is not the traditional type of doctors' office. What has happened? As I continue with my inspection of the place, my ears are trying to tune in with the neo-soul music playing very softly from the Bose speakers that I see appointed to each end of the room. My nose starts to twitch and tingle from the smell lavender incense burning. This place has a very calming effect. The lighting in the office is relaxing, and it is not too bright. Now this is how a doctor's office should look, and smell. I have now entered the NO STRESS ZONE! Damn, please tell me they got a shoe rack in this place. I am ready to get comfortable!

"Mrs. Jones?"

"How you doing baby?" she says while extending her arms wide open. Now this woman is a handful. She is so sweet, she reminds me of my own grandmother.

"What have you all done with the suite?" I quizzed, while taking in the spectacular view.

"Oh we decided to give the office an at home theme."

"Really, what made you all do that?"

"The doctor really came to understand one true meaning."

"What's that?" I asked while trying to hover over this woman as if she was giving me the secret to *real* happiness.

"You have to spend money in order to make money child!" as she did a three snaps, a twist *and* a dip!

"Please don't have me screaming up in this place, Miss. Jones!"

"That damn doctor has really been spending money lately. I got to get him while he feeling good honey!"

"Well, he just needs to listen to you and he will be all right!"

"That man doesn't ever listening to a shit I say." Ms. Jones yells as she shakes her head in pure disgust.

"You can fix him. Just keep on his ass. However, I can say he is a good doctor though. I feel so much better, since I have been coming here. The best part is that I have not ever had to fill a prescription for meds."

"Yeah he really doesn't like to prescribe meds unless the patient is REALLY off the chain!"

"You crack me up Mrs. Jones, what you know bout being 'off the chain'?"

"Why you young folks think us old folks dead? She asked while placing her hands on her hips. I could see we was about to go up to another level with this conversation.

"Okay, I'll send your '*street credit'* card in the mail, in case you get flagged by some young thang on the streets." I teased.

"Okay, Miss Thang, let's get back to business." She instructs, while pushing me towards her desk as if I am some kid late for class.
She checks her calendar with a concentrated glare over her gold trimmed, *Essence* eyewear.

"I see you right here Mrs. Lewis. The doctor is running a few minutes behind, but he has a suite ready for you, follow me please."

"Look at you, being all professional and shit!" I teased.

"Child please, hushes yo mouth! You knows he be on my head about getting too personal with patients." She playfully stated in her old pushed to the side southern tone of voice.

"Dang, I was ready to chill in the waiting area. The music is on hit and the aroma of french vanilla and hazelnuts is a treat all by itself. I love the new office theme; I know you had about what, a hundred percent in the say-so of this change."

"You know I run this office!" she laughed.

Mrs. Jones is so nice. I loved how she always styled her African gowns, and headdresses. I do not know who is caring for her locks, but she could surely stand a visit to my salon. Maybe I will slip her one of my cards, offer a free "do" and see what happens from there. She totally fits the theme of this office. Neo-Africa is what I call it. A little bit of old school vibe mixed with the essence, beauty, and royalty of Africa. She seems to love her job, and does not appear to be judgmental or nosy as to why I am here. That is what I call doing your job. Simply minding your own damn business is a job that many people should try applying for on a full-time basis.

"Please feel free to relax, flip through some magazines, or treat your self to the refreshment cart inside the suite, the doctor will be in shortly. There is a restroom on the left side of the suite, if you need one."

"Like I don't know where it's at boss lady." I responded, while trying my best not to bug up at her so-called act of professionalism.

She swiftly walks away.

"Thank you." I sang out as she closes the door.

I see not much has changed in the decorating process in regards to the doc's office. I guess he told Mrs. Jones that his office was *NOT* apart of the *operation up-grade* project. Oh well, I may as well take another tour his office.

The music continues to play throughout the entire office, and suddenly I hear my favorite song come on overhead and I instantly start to swing my wide and curvy hips to the sultry and seductive rhythms of Raheem DeVaughns' latest hit; *"YOU."* That man knows he can sing notes right off of sheet music into the Music Hall of Fame! The way he rocks a song, will make you feel like he is singing to you the whole way through. He can whisper a sweet chord of love into my ears anytime. I cannot even count the number of times that CD has been in rotation inside my car, my salon *and* at home. I am surprised it has not melted into any of my CD players.

I still have a few minutes before the good doctor shows up, I guess I can go to the restroom to admire myself once again, and then finish taking in the ambiance of this beautiful suite. Stepping out of the restroom, I pause to take notice at how this brother man has the most exceptional taste. I peep out the cherry colored, leather chaise across the room. I felt myself drawn to the chaise, as a pencil is to paper.

I stretched my goddess like frame out across the chaise. The leather is firm, but not to the point where it pinches me. I lean back, and next thing I know I find myself ready to tell my whole life story to a stranger I barely know anything about. Later, I wake up and I noticed that ten more minutes have passed, and no doctor has shown up. Now why is he going to make me flash my bitch license?

All the shit I go through to find a good therapist and this damn man has nerve enough to be late for *my* appointment! This is the reason why I jumped around to so many doctors. They can never keep up with their appointments. He should know there is a *"V.I.P."* (I will explain about V.I.P. in a few) waiting on him.

A few seconds later, the knock I was awaiting thundered through the wooden door.

"May I enter the room Mrs. Lewis?" The doctor asks.

"Yes, you can."

"Hello, Dr. Phillips."

"You feel good today?" The doctor asks while carrying a stack of orange folders.

"Why are you fucking playing with me, Ray?"

"Excuse me?" he asks, as he turns to make sure the door closed.

"Don't worry, I'll lock the door."

While keeping my good eye on the doctor I glided towards his office door and clicked the lock. I am trying very hard to show this man, what his so-called *therapy* has done for me over the last three months.

"You know, I've been coming here for a while now and I just can't seem to get my feelings under control Ray. What do you think is the problem?"

"I can start off with a number of things, but I think you know better than I do Mrs. Lewis. I'll give you a few moments to tell me what is *really* bothering you." By looking at his body language, his writing on his tablet becomes faster and more intense. Secondly, he doesn't even make eye contact with me at all. I guess this is going to be a long session. His mind must be in other places today. He really doesn't know what a great job he has done of preparing the stage for my debut.

"For months I've come to you in search of finding my true self. I feel as if I am missing some thing..."

I cannot help but to notice that he is smiling his ass off. I know I have not said a damn thing funny either. If one more asshole laughs at me when I am talking and I have not said shit funny...I am trying out for the Def Jam Comedy Show!

"Sorry for the silly look, my mind is really occupied with a lot of things today Mrs. Lewis." The doctor stated, in a very *'this is what it is'* type of manner.

"Fuck all this staged playtime shit, get rid of the secretary for the day and lets do what we need to do. I hate when the *other me* comes out. What I may do next, may not be pretty for anyone else to see or hear." I confessed.

"Rae, I think we need to stop and take the time to talk about a few things."

"No we don't and here... is the reason why!" I yelled, while pushing the good doctor back down into his leather wing back chair with my foot.

I opened my black, silky Christian Dior wrap dress to give the doctor the view he had been waiting on. I hate it when a brother tries to put my hot ass on ice!

He reaches for the intercom button, and I quickly grab hold of his hand. My six-carat diamond bracelet was sun struck, which was blinding to us both. I re-adjust my grip to make sure the good doctor could see my face when I talk my talk.

"Use caution when dealing with me Ray. Without me in your life, you will feel that you have made the worst choice ever! Be smart and make the right choice. I promise you'll want to schedule me for *more* endless sessions before this one is even over."

He acts before he thinks, which tells me I have total control. Like the trainer has over a lion. The only difference: I need no whip to train this fine beast of a man.

"Mrs. Jones... Could you please retrieve those files I requested, and sit them in my research area? Take the rest of the day off. I'll be conducting research for the rest of the day after I visit with Mrs. Lewis."

"Thank you very much doctor. Is there anything else you want me to do before leaving the office sir?"

"No, just lock the suite up when you leave."

I can hear that woman ripping and running around the office preparing to leave. She jetted out of the office as if she was already ten minutes into overtime *and* she was about to miss her bus ride home.

"I'm so surprised in your choice Ray..." He holds up his hand, cutting me off as if he had some big announcement to make.

"Look Desirae, you talk to me, as if I have no say so in our relationship. You do not know the real me! Why would you want to continue with this? You are a married woman with a beautiful child and the successful owner of several day spas and salons. Not to mention the fact you hold a much-respected name in the community. The position you hold is about as high as a ride on an elephant through the safari jungles of Africa. You're riding high, but at what cost do you want to risk that ride to cease; only to be delivered to the wild hyenas of the safari?" He quizzes while he is rolling up his sleeves and giving me the utmost serious look ever.

"Baby, I have some thing to tell you." I whined, trying not to show how eager I am to mount this man and become one with him like *real* lovers do.

"What is it Rae?"

"I'm crazy in love with you. I felt it from the first day our lips met. There was something far more than lust, attraction or any other evident reason. I feel we have been to some of the same places in this journey of life and now all I want to do is to lay with you for the rest of my life baby. I'm tired and I just need someone I really love to be with for all of eternity. I admitted my mistakes to you, along with many more. I got married for all the wrong reasons Ray." *I feel so crazy for telling him all of this, when he hasn't told me that much about his life.*

"Baby, come on! I can't take this right now. I got too much on my mind right now. I think that is your pussy talking Rae! When did you start really thinking about making a change like this?" Ray ponders.

Why is he not giving me eye contact today? I can't understand why he has this sudden need to withdraw from me on today of all days! The day good old Rae decides to make her pussy available to only one man; he treats me like a melted Popsicle. He can't lick on me a few times and throw me away!

"I know this is a lot to take in, but it was *you*, who wanted me to leave. You have always stated how unhealthy as well as, how unsafe living a life of lies and deceit could be. I just want all of this to blow up (if it must) then let the smoke clear and we roll on with life from there." I pleaded.

"You got this shit figured out already, huh?" he asks while blankly staring at the floor as he nervously bit on his fingernails.

"Hey, I'm done hiding, how about you?" I asked, while backing up from up him. Suddenly the feeling of betrayal covers my body.

"Damn baby, you mean to tell me you are ready to make the move huh?" Ray asked.

"What is the problem Ray?" I asked while fixing my dress and combing my fingers through my hair.

I noticed he seems to be quite apprehensive about talking to me today. He must have had a bad start, or maybe it could be family issues (that he never seems to want to talk about) occupying his mind. He is nervous, shaky and very un-coordinated, which is totally opposite to the smooth and debonair man I know of.

"Baby there is so much shit on my mind I really don't know where to start." Ray confesses while he looks at me with those delicious key lime colored eyes.

"Well you know what?" I purred out.

"What?"

"Start here." I said as I pointed to my pelvic region. A region, he traveled upon way too many times to count. I know he can never turn down a trip of ecstasy inside my *pelvic region.*

"Damn, girl you never cease to amaze me. How can you think of fucking at a time like this?" he questions while massaging his dick.

"What? Don't act like a good hit of this won't make your blues go away Ray!" I teased while I rubbed on my pussy."

"Let me see how wet she is." Ray demanded as he hungrily licked his lips.

Off went the six-inch candy red Prada stilettos that I picked up at the mall yesterday in anticipation of this "therapy session" with the good doctor. Before I even had the chance to remove, my bra brother man was out of his slacks and underwear. The only thing he had left on was his shirt and a sinful smile. His shirt was wide-open, showing off his washboard abs. He sat on top of his desk with his legs cocked slightly to the position of ten till two! Fuck a watch, this is good timing right here!

"Damn baby you give an excellent view!" I screamed out while I gently rubbed between my thick thighs, giving him some hella tempting eye candy. He loves to watch me play with my pussy.

The view he left was just enough for me to view what I had ahead of me! Every time we get to this point, I have to stop, reflect and wonder if I am woman enough for all of this man to be inside of me! The fact that he was exceptionally long and hard today made my pause even longer. His shit was on point more than any other day I had seen before. Maybe it was the news of leaving my husband that got him and "his boy" all excited.

"Come here baby!" he commanded.

He grabbed me by my arm, pulled me closer and placed his lips on my neck, sucking and licking upon my neck as if his favorite dessert lay upon it. I felt as if I received powerful injections of lust at a 20,000cc's, and fiery desire, given at 10,000cc's. Hell, a high dosage of any drug given in those amounts would be enough to kill any human being. The powerful injections of lust and desire, massaged and constricted my veins, raised all my body hairs, and had my nerves on vibrate! The feeling of pleasure was upon me, I started to melt right onto this man, and he had not even made his entrance.

"Desirae, what is this we are doing? I *know* this is more than lust and pure attraction, but how will this end for us?" Ray questions.

I do not need him interrupting my vibe, by saying some shit that will make the mood die out like a car battery in the dead of winter. Hell, even if that happens I got enough juice to give him the jump he needs.

"Please, no talking during this *session*. Just show me! This *is, "The Show Me State"* after all. Don't disappoint me Ray."

There we were, laid out on his supple cherry colored chaise. I deeply gazed into his eyes, and dived into his mouth like a seasoned Olympic diver to retrieve his tongue. The kissing was so sensuous to the point where no breathing took place, but yet our hearts kept on beating and we didn't tire out. His hands rolled up and down my backside as if he was painting a masterpiece. I could feel my muscles melt right into his palms.

"Okay it's time for the condom, we can't get too caught up…just slow down!" I barked out.

I pulled the Magnum condom from underneath my bracelet band (yes …I DON"T PLAY, I try to be prepared at all times; even though I have slipped a few times before), and opened the package with my teeth!

His dick rose right up between my thighs as if it were looking for warmth and shelter. I placed the condom on him, as if his dick was the next Prince in line waiting to be crowned King. Next, I reached down and moved my silky red Gucci panties over to allow his dick to slide right on in, as if it was fighting for this special parking spot all day long.

"Umm your shit is too warm and wet; don't get mad if I slam on in Desirae. I have no fuel in my brake line, and stopping would be impossible right now. There has to be a little work done before I can start to smooth things on out in order to start the *long hard ride* to your place of pleasure." He growled as he slid himself deep within me, while playing with my clit.

Oh, I love it when he talks dirty and role-plays. I'm feeling so good now I can't even move my tongue to allow words of admiration and praise to flow. All I can do is roll my eyes and my neck around to give him a nod of the feelings being mutual. The first few moments of where *it* slips inside of me are the best. It is that point where *warmness meets stiffness.* It gives a completely new meaning to "head butting".

"Please baby, stroke it smoothly and slowly, don't rush with this today. It's me and you today." I chanted as I desperately begged him to love me long and slowly.

"You weren't expecting this type of treat today were you Ray? I mean I just had to have you from the moment I saw you in the physician directory. Your still lips from the photo, were whispering a story to me a story that I just had to hear." I said as I wrapped my arms around his body and hugged it tightly.

"I never knew our relationship would take off to this level. I know I'm very much attracted to men that have power. I really don't know you as well as I like, but this has to go on. You're feeling too good to me right now, and I know there has to be more of you, and I want it all."
He smiles back.

"Baby, we're going make this shit work." He promised, while running his soft hands through my hair, as he gently kissed upon my face and full breast.

I can't help but to stare at this man. I am in total awe. Six-foot five, a solid muscular frame, and eyes the color of deeply sun-ripened kiwi. With teeth so white, and perfectly aligned, I'm tempted to believe that they're veneers. His lips are full and luscious looking. *Ooh, there is that shiver again.*
His hair is so curly, but not to the point where it looks nappy. It is a natural, almost an exotic look for him. Ray's skin has the appearance of freshly wrapped caramel- just unwrap and eat! How yummy.

"This sex is intense, have it your way Desirae."

From there the super freak appears. I turn on top of him while he lays flat on his back, now my back is facing him, but I'm still riding him, like the cowgirl I am. Hell, the only thing missing is my lasso, and cowgirl hat. I lean forward on my hands, and I look back only to see this man melting into his of his chaise. He is looking up to the ceiling as if he was thanking God he came to work today, and not attending some dumb meeting or convention. I rise up and down; fast one minute slow the next, while my ass claps on his lower abdomen. The tease in me suddenly comes out. I slide my wetness all the way down to his shaft then all the way back to his tip at the slowest rate I possibly can. His fat mushroomed shaped head is one any woman would want inside of her. No matter what it taps against, you will feel its effect.

"The head is all I need to work baby in order to make your own head that sits between your shoulders explode!" He is trying to catch his breath, while reaching out for me.

"Damn woman, there has to be a river down there! I can't take this, I'm drowning and I really don't know how long I can hold out!" Ray cried while still trying his best to lift me off him, before he *lets* go. I slow down to allow him to regain himself so he will not release.

"Oh not now baby… I want to finish this ride as well, hold it in!" I spin around on his flagpole of a penis, and I pull my breast out.

"Here baby, suck on these breasts, instead of releasing inside these walls!"

He takes to my tits like a mad man. Damn I love how his tongue feels warm and slithery with just enough fuzz and wetness on it to make my nipples rock up as if I was standing outside in the dead of winter with no shirt on.

Damn, where does he take titty -sucking classes? My own husband can't suck, and lick on my breast like this! Ray certainly has a way of making me feel. Suddenly I feel exhaustion, but not any sooner than I feel a climax coming on.

"Ray... now *I* can't hold out and I feel all of my insides running your all down you!" I exclaim!

He smiles.

"Well then I'll meet you in the middle."

At this moment, I am so glad that damn secretary of his left, because the cows were out grazing the fields. One moan belted out right after one another, until there was complete silence.

I blow back the hair that shielded my face, while I tried to recuperate from our *sexual* therapy.

"I'm panting too hard, like I just finished a race or some thing. Damn baby, you let it out today!"

I am looking around for water, but to be truthful there is no need for refreshments. I am so tempted to say something so silly, because the sex was awesome! You ever get it so good that you say some silly shit (that you love, like, or hell never even tried before) like...,"HOT BISCIUTS AND GRAVY!" or something like "I LOVE YO MOMMA!" Well shit, that is how good this dick was!

"This is what I was talking about, damn that was more than refreshing than cold bottled Fiji water on a hot summers day. My thirst has been quenched!" I proclaimed as I did my victory hump on top of him.

"I'm sure you really didn't expect any of this, but it is what it is Ray."

Taking note of the time, a quick surge of panic comes over me.

"Hell, I can't get my clothes on fast enough. I'm running late for my noon client, I'll just have to freshen up at the salon when I make it there."

"Desirae, I really need take the time to think about what happened today, because if I continue to see you… hell forget it, I can't even think right. At this moment I can't find the words even if there was a dictionary sitting right here in front of me." I smile, and take his words as a compliment. As I gathered my things and head to the door, he almost knocks me over in attempt to block my exit.

With his large biceps fully extended from one end of the doorway to the other, he looks me dead into my eyes with the most sincere look ever.

"I'll see you on Monday, from ten until three. I know you don't serve clients on Mondays, so I'll see you then."

I smiled, because once again I was right. *See my V.I.P. (very important pussy) was what I had waiting on him. I hate a man to keep me on ice. This pussy is so hot that when it gets puts on ice: the ice itself melts and then I have to go invest in some fucking new panties.*

I had him right where I wanted him. My strut to through door was a proud, confident, victorious and (even though I thought I was going to fall on my face from me having jelly legs) sexy one. I flipped my long, silky honey blonde hair over my shoulder striking a very sexy pose from my good side. I spoke one last time to the good doctor.

"Hey Ray…it's time to step up or move on. I want to put everything on the table on Monday. You ready for that?"

"Can I eat everything on that succulent table spread of yours?" Ray ponders in a very silly, and joking matter.

"Quit playing with me!" I hate when he tries to be funny, because really...he's not.

I know he is feeling me because I can remember way back when I first started my seducing act and he was trying to keep his composure. Proved out he was weaker than a rack of fucking lambs! I instantly started to laugh as I thought back to our early days. Next thing I knew I was laughing so hard tears came to the corner of my eyes.

"What's funny Rae?" Ray asks in a defensive tone of voice.

"Just thinking about the day when you tried to turn me away!"

"Huh?" he asks while trying not to look like busted out.

"Ray, can you remember anything without referring to your notes?"

I took a few steps towards him and then leaned into his ear.

"Tell me what I told you when I tried to show you the *regions*, for the first time."

The bright blush to his face gave light to the fact that he remembered our first session of lovemaking.

"Mrs. Lewis my code of ethics, along with the doctor/patient rules I have in place won't allow me to...," he growled out.

"What doctor?" I whined

"Well let me whisper those sweet nothings into your ear." I purred as I leaned over Ray's shoulder.

"Your rules won't allow you to take your hands, and rub them up and down my swollen, but yet tender thighs? Will those rules allow you to hold onto my long strong hair, hold me from a distance, then slowly pull me towards you, so that all of your "hard" love slides in, and out through this wet wonder? If not, then you need to change those rules! I will allow you to do that and even more. Don't worry, I won't charge you." I slowly grinded each word out.

"What did I do after that Ray?" I asked while I had placed my hands over his eyes, so he could have a clear re-play of our first session in the dark.

Cheesing from ear to ear he slowly spoke.

"You started walking towards me and I stepped back... you paused, then you proceeded, but for some reason I was frozen stiff."

"Yeah, I knew I had you when your body motioned a sign of sweet of surrender. Your lips got very wet, and your eyes tried to focus in on as much as you could get inside those tiny pupils. I could see the desire your eyes so much that your pupils turned from light green to an intense fiery red."

"Yeah" he responds, as he lets out a deep, Barry White sounding type of growl.

"How did you know you had me Rae?"

"When I opened my dress and showed you your new home!" I said as I fell onto his solid frame while looking him directly in his eyes.

"You were trying not to look, but your eyes were locked and loaded like an M-16 assault rifle. You were ready to fire out them rounds. I noticed how your eyes gazed at my goddess like body as if it were on display like a fine piece of exquisite art in a museum. I decided my outfit was the right one. Easy on and easy off! I just couldn't decide the pose of seduction I was going to be in, until I got into your office. Sister has to check out the stage before she puts on a show!" I said while I provocatively danced before him.

"Don't even try to act like you didn't feel all that tension between us!" I stated for the damn record.

"Baby, all I can say is that I hope you really mean what you are saying. I'm praying that you are really ready to find out about me and I can only anticipate that you will be able to accept some good and not so good things about me."

"I love you Ray, we can do all things as love as we truly love and believe in one another."

"Bye babe." he whispers.

I love the way he kisses my forehead without making me feel like he is giving me that "best-gal pal" kiss. This is truly moving towards the right direction.

I am aware that my life may soon be taking the turn down that detoured road momma warned me not to take. Sometimes, there never seems to be any other "open roads" while you are in route to what you think is true happiness.

~Chapter 4~

Break it Down

Why am I running? I do not hear any sirens. "Get it together girlfriend, you have done this act in extreme excess. No need to act as if it is your first time."

I smile and then I push the unlock button on my remote to allow me into my car. The mirror is in the same position I left it in, **RIGHT IN MY FACE!** I stare right back at it, studying what type of person I really am. I can't think straight now. I am still in awe of what I just experienced. My heart beats fast, but only because I am scared (why should I be?) now. I can't figure out why I love having sexual escapades, with so many different men. I'm married to a good man, yet, it's not enough! I look around to see who is on the parking lot, and I see no one is there to view me in my moment of shame.

"Okay, that moment is over." Like I've said, it is what it is and life goes on. I notice the time and I start up my ride to jet off to the salon. Fuck! This man has no sense of timing at all! I guess I had better answer his call now. I can hear him crying right now, "I know you screen your calls and I *know* you saw me calling you, so why didn't you pick up Rae?" Who in the hell said you had to pick up the phone on the first, second or third ring? No answer means call back, right?

"Hey, Lance making money or talking money?" I ask. All I hear is silence.

"Hello?" No reply came through.

"Look, Lance quit playing on the phone!" I hate when my calls drop! A familiar voice finally starts to break through.

"Sorry baby for putting you on hold, right after I called you; this guy called me right back and I was finally able to convince him that he was getting a great deal on the Conway house for one point four million.

"Lance, you call that a deal?" He starts laughing.

"You know the area baby, if that's what they want, and they got the cash; well then I got their house keys waiting. Look, sweetness I simply called you to see how the appointment went for you this morning."

Why this motherfucker acting like, we didn't blow up on each other like Iraq this morning?

"I really want you to come home tonight so we can talk. That appointment must have gone well, you sound very happy!"

Does he really want to know how it went? In and out real slow, if I could tell him the truth. Damn, there goes that shiver again.

"The doctor kind of pissed me off by running late, but once he made his entrance I... I mean *we* were finally able to get on the ball."

I better not slip and say the wrong damn thing. Sometimes my mouth gets ahead of my mind.

"By the way, you never told me the location or the name of this doctor baby. You have been going for a while and I want to meet this doctor."

"Doctor Archibald Reynolds!" I quickly blurted out.

I must have my shit on point at all times. It's funny how the main dog can "sniff" out another dog on his turf. They start acting all funny, running around in circles panting with their tongues hanging out! What stupid looking animals. I decided to have another doctor on backup, just incase Lance got too nosy.

"Well Rae, is there anything we need to talk about as husband and wife at this doctors office? Will there be an invitation for me to come in and sit in for a session?

Damn, I'm trying to imagine us all in a threesome. I don't think Lance could handle the fact of seeing me ride up and down on Ray like the first black woman of Rodeo! I mean the way I rode that man, was the kind of ride that you do after you've been with someone for a while, not after five or six *"lust fucks."* You just do not start fucking strangers like you been with them your whole life. That shit rarely happens. It is as if I knew Rays' body. I instantly laughed aloud because that thought alone tickled my mind!

"Did I say something funny Rae?" he asks sounding more irritated than concerned about my "mental" health.

I instantly snapped back.

"Look Lance, give me some time! The doctor did mention that eventually he would love to bring you in. Getting to know you, as well as hearing you voice your concerns, are very important to him in regards to my healing process. Right now, it is all about me. I think we are at the stage to where he is trying to show me that I can trust him. That he's there to help me make better choices in my life and not judge me. That's what I like about him Lance. Unlike all the other "*textbook PhD's*" you had me to visit!" I hoped that my explanation would not only calm Lance down, but show him that I'm eager to fix my *so-called* problems.

"Dr. Reynolds is not into judging. He sits back and takes whatever I give him." In addition, he's not quick to prescribe me the latest tranquilizing drug on the market. I hated how those meds made me feel. I couldn't keep up with shit and I was always *too* mellow and sleeping a lot! That's not how I fucking roll. If that's the case, just prescribe me some weed and let me enjoy the shit!" Hell, the last time I remember, those damn anti-depressants had me living life in slow motion! Every thing was such a delay for me and everything was a fucking drag! A motherfucker could have told me I was being sued, my Benz caught on fire and all my stylists walked out all my salons, and my response would be; "Wow. Okay, call me later; I need to take a nap!"

"Well excuse me for caring. I just wanted to make sure that you will be able to get help with an issue that not only I see, but other members of our family, and even some of your employees."

I had to pull the car over now. This asshole is starting that shit up again.

"Wait Lance, what are you talking about friends and family have issues with my attitude. "Once again, and I state for the fucking record that no one has ever stepped to me; or even hinted towards the fact that they have an issue with me. Who in the hell have you been talking to in my camp? I thought we respected each other enough to stay out of each others business, unless we brought it home."

"Look baby, I do mind my business but when your employees feel the need to talk to me about your behavior, or your own child does not want to involve you in some of the things that she does, then don't you feel that there is something wrong?"

Shit, I am feeling a lot and at this moment, it sure as hell is not him. I do believe it is a little of Ray's "creamy mayo" sliding out of my panties all down my thighs. Damn, Ray must have broken the condom again. Is there a bigger condom? I cannot afford slip-ups like this!

"Lance you know what type of woman I am. Business is business. I cater to my clients. I make sure that everyone who visits the salon has an experience that exceeds his or her expectations at all times. When it comes to my employees, they need to be high gear and ready to serve the people that; keep our lights on, pay our mortgages and keeps us all in decent transportation. I have zero tolerance for people that take the easy road, or look for pampering along the way. I do not have time when people bullshit me either. While they are busy running to you (*as if I did not know who the snakes were)* did they mention all the shit they have been doing? Was there any mentioning of being late, fucking up client's hair, not having my entire booth rent ready and on time?"

Oh, now he's quite and shit now!

"Baby there is always two sides to an issue, and I guess I should have talked to you first, instead of sitting you out in the rain to get poured on like that. Rae, I may not be current on all that is going on with your business, but I can tell you that I have noticed a change on a personal level about you for a while now. I'm not sure what it is, but I really don't like it." I am tired of talking to him now!

"Look Lance, we need to talk about this face to face at home tonight. Send Rachel over to your parents and we can talk about this tonight. Just when I think all is well Lance, you spring some more new shit out on me. Be ready to talk tonight!" I slammed my flip phone shut so hard; I just knew I had to order another one. Whatever happened to sticking by one another? It seems as if he wanted to hear all the negative shit about me and go straight to the jury without a trial. This marriage is really in need of some quick dissolve. It is time for me to face the music in regards to my marriage.

I can't believe he talked to me about the same bullshit like that! He thinks he is so perfect. Lance has no faults. It is my entire fault, I forgot! Like last nights dishwater, the thought of having a great day has gone down the drain.

I can't get to the shop fast enough now. My only dilemma is how do I go to work? What will my mode be today? I am about ready to make some changes in my *entire* life. Everyone in that salon knows no one is to step to anyone that is not an employee, or owner of Simple Pleasures Day Spas and Salons, with inside issues! "OK girl, gather yourself together, this is your business. It is simply time to clean house and tighten the reins until they stop completely, and recognize that I am the boss and they are the employees." I can't be too drastic though. No one needs to know that I am aware that there is a snitch in my camp.

I walk into the shop and suddenly it gets quite. Shit, are all these bitches on the same page or what? I cannot have this type of shit lying right under my nose. All I wanted to do was get fresh and change, but I see business needed tending to.

"Good morning ladies. I hope I didn't interrupt anything going on in *my* shop!" I hear a snicker, but the bitch is not smart enough to stand out and do it.

"Okay girls, finish your current client and cancel your appointments for the rest of the day! I have a few Celebes coming in this evening, and they want the spa for their entourage and themselves. A couple of new school divas, called in at the last minute, and has informed me that they will be requiring our services. Their stylists will not be here to prepare them for their meeting with the press tonight. We have to whip those do's up! Their stylists will not be in town until late tomorrow evening and it will be too late to whip their hair into shape. I am sorry *'honey bunnies'* about this last minute notice. We hardly get requests like this, but when they come, we have to step up to the occasion.

Lila I will need you here to entertain as well as serve the food and drinks. Bella I will need you on Janet's' hair. I know you will be able to rock it like the concert they plan on throwing this weekend girlfriend."

The snipping of the scissors stop, the blow dryers die out and their hands become posted firmly on their hips!

"Excuse me Desirae, but how you just gone make us cancel our appointments for the day! Damn, you arrive here late, in your own world it seems, humming like you don't have a single care in the world, you..."

"Look... first of all I called my client to inform her that my arrival time would be delayed, and I gave her the option of staying or rescheduling; and she re-scheduled. Secondly, you fired, and third leave NOW! I will have your shit delivered by Fed-Ex to your house. Do you really think you can talk to me like this in my shop in front of clients, in this type of unprofessional manner Janelle?"

I was happy to get rid of this bitch Janelle. She thinks she runs this salon ***and*** my assistant, Lila. Lila has had too many problems with her following directions when given. Not to mention the fact the bitch cannot even style hair. My daughter does a better job styling her American Girl Dolls hair. Rachel styles her dolls hair when I do not have time to style them, or take her to the American Girl Doll Shop in Chicago for our girls' day out sprees.

I gave Janelle a chance. My head stylist Carmen left here, to run my New York, salon. My friend Kendall who managed the NY salon, moved to Paris, to be with her fiancé. There, it is just that fucking simple.

"Ladies, it's time for a meeting, send your clients to the lounge area, and meet me in my office within five minutes! Give your clients a complementary coupon for the café, until we are finished with our business."

I can't hold it in any more; this playground shit has to stop. One by one, the clicker of heels and the shuffles of tennis shoes only made me more anxious to line them all up one by one and shoot them down in no particular order! Hell if it was that easy, they should all have their own salons. Why is it that the troublemakers, never own their own shit? I guess the idea of fucking up other peoples shit, instead of his or her own is a sweet one to cherish.

"It has come to my attention that there seems to be some individuals that have issues with my behavior/attitude. I want this shit out on the table like food at a picnic. I want you to mention what it really is that is making you women feel so *stressed*. Please feel free to talk. Everyone knows that whatever happens here in the salon stays. We do not involve the outside with the inside. We are here to care for our clients, and give them the best treatment possible."

These bitches are scary. Not one of them is even thinking about breathing as I carry on with my military version of a *shakedown*.

"People visit our salon because it is their refuge; it is their place to come let it all out, to complain, to vent, to cry, and to do whatever makes them feel good. Shit... we are therapists with a fucking HOTCOMB! We listen, we give advice, and sometimes the best thing we can do is... SHUT THE FUCK UP! Sometimes the advice is not good enough and sometimes it is. We teach them to use their intuition as well as their hearts. That is all apart of being a woman. What I do not feel is when women cannot speak their mind, and tell the truth while doing it! I mean if I am wrong, show me and let me start apologizing!" I pleaded as I raised my restless hands into the air.

I pause just to see who has something to say. Nothing but pure silence leans against the rooms four walls!

"Okay, one more time for me to ask what the deal is before I make my announcement." Silence again.

"I'll inform you ladies in the morning who will have a job here and who won't. When I hired you women, I instructed you all about the rules of conduct. I gave you all handbooks, and informative packets with your contracts. All of this paperwork is located inside your files along with your personal progress reports as a stylist here at the salon. Let me simply state, you termination will occur if you are below standards, and if I have caught you in any violation of policies here at the salon. Be prepared for that delivery from Fed-Ex. Suddenly, they all get that puzzled look that kids have on their faces at a magic show: "Gee how can she do that?"

"Rae, you are tripping out girl." Shelitha responded while popping the hell out of her gum.

"Well don't worry cause I got plenty tricks up my sleeves and the show isn't finished yet! I asked you all what the deal is and none of you had shit to say, so this talk is finished." I shouted back while widening my eyes.

"Leave my office, finish your current client, and leave. I will see you all here in the morning." The clicker of the heels and the shuffling of tennis shoes seemed to move a little slower now. I look up and I see one person (I am surprised) standing in my presence.

"Lila what do you need?"

"Desirae, I'm concerned about you. You seem to have too much on your plate. I try my best to help by arranging your meetings, watching the shop, and tending to some of the financial matters of the shop. You are extending yourself too much. One can only stretch only so far before they rip into a million little pieces. You have salons in New York, Chicago, California *and* here in St. Louis. Do you ever feel exhausted? All of this stress is affecting the way you talk and respond to people Rae. Do you miss Lance, and Rachel? Have I struck a nerve with all the questions? You really need to take some time off Rae. Get back in touch with yourself and your family as well."

Okay, I feel like Ike Turner right about now. Remember the part from the movie *"What's Love Got to Do with It?"* when Ike asked:

"You, said what? You…trying to help IKE?" as he mumbled out, while he does his dope head stumble.

At that moment Tina about had to shit out about fifty bricks in the recording booth, because she knew an ass whipping was close. I loved that movie. Lawrence and Angela, hell the whole world knew they should have gotten an award for their roles. I stood up from behind my desk, and I gave Lila a very intense stare. Surprisingly, she stood her ground.

"Look Lila, let me explain something to you. I made it to the point in which I am standing because I handled my business. I was the one who rose before the sun acting upon my plans and goals that I had thought of on the previous night. You will learn that in business, failure is no ones fault but your own. Trust me, when you fail, someone else succeeds. That is why I am always doing majority of things on my own. I don't need a front man or woman to run my operation. You should be happy to be on my team as my assistant. Furthermore, I don't need you checking me on my personal life either. I see my husband and daughter just enough, thank you!"

"Desirae, we go way back! Why do you have to act like this with me?" she whines out as she desperately tries to gain eye contact with me.

"Hey Lila this is business, and that is the way I want to keep things! I don't give a damn how far we go back, you had better understand, that outside shit does not work inside my place of business! You are here to do a job. Either you can do the job for which I hired you to do, or you can leave! Do not ever cross me, or lie to me! I promise you won't like how I respond to betrayal!"

I cannot seem to pace myself now, because I am feeling the tears swell in my eyes, and I am trying not to shake. All I want to do is to kick her ass right now!

"Please don't worry your little head; I'm sure you have plenty of things on your mind Desirae. This I can promise you though. When I leave, you will know it, because your world will be at its end. The end will come when your life and all of its burdens will be too much for you to bear. I have listened to you and this ***"NINO BROWN, THE WORLD IS MINE!"*** type of attitude excessively long. When you come down off whatever you are on, and the door hits you in your face ***real hard*** about a million times, and God finally shows himself to you, don't come crying to me. I am all you got! Don't ever think Lila Anderson is soft and sleeping light bitch!"

I stood back to my feet, because in the Lou---the word 'bitch' equals a fight!

"Love you like a sis, but you needed to be put in your place. Think about what I SAID, and trust that I will be here tonight... once again, to help your sorry ass out!" With all that said, Lila's petite, but yet strong and solid frame high tailed it out of my office and slammed my fucking door.

Was I just *'punked'*, or given a wake up call to hear some shit I needed to hear? Damn, girlfriend did grow some balls! Oh well, I guess by her speech and her true concern for my life, I can continue to count on her. That girl has skin like a dragon, she may be hurt, but she will heal very quickly.

I know the girl loves me like a sister. I love her as well. It's so hard to find a girlfriend that will not get jealous, not want to fuck your man and not leave your side when the real shit goes down. However, I still felt it was necessary to put her in place regarding the use of our friendship as a quick escape route for her to do what she wants, when she wants. People will have a field day if they knew that Lila and I go back. I treat everyone of these girls as equals. I don't need anyone trying to sue me over some bullshit. I forgot how hood that girl could be!

Okay now I have the chance to freshen up from my morning rendez-vous. What will I do about the good doctor? Should I continue seeing him or should the relationship end? I am feeling the man in me come out now because my pussy is telling me to keep fucking...I mean keep-receiving therapy from the good doctor. I just hope he does not pull on the wrong handle on my emotions and open the portal to hell.

I lock my office door, and decide to have a seat to think about the day's events before I shower. I can't help but to think about Ray. *Oh Lord, there is that shiver again.*

I hate using the Lord's name when I am being so bad, but the Lord is so good that I guess I am saying thank you, in a messed up kind of way. Rays' image flashes before me, and all I can do is spin around in my chair, while I massage my pussy. Damn I can't take it. I stop spinning in the chair; take off my dress as well as my panties. I sit back down, place each foot over the arms of my chair, and I vigorously play with my clit like a violinist working the strings. Up and down, side to side.

"Work it, work it, now hold it right there, and DAMN!" The symphony is complete. Now if only I can lift my legs and be able to walk to the shower without busting my ass wide open onto this marble floor, I'll be cool.

Keeping your friends close and your enemies closer is harder to do when you are not sure who's who!

~Chapter 5~

Rae's Way

Oh my damn, I can't believe the time we had! Ms. J and Ms, B, was more than what I expected them to be. Don't get me wrong, I knew these sisters had their shit on point, but these women were on a level higher than the sky itself. They truly are stars. They have a spirit, and inner glow that deserves to be in the sky to shine. My hands hurt so badly from all that weaving I did. I never saw so much hair covering my salon floor.

I was right, Bella lit into Ms. J's' hair. That girl is my best stylist. She knows how to capture the essence of a woman and highlight on it. She never goes outside the boundaries. That girl is going places. I know after the type of treatment that Ms. B. and Ms, J, had received: I felt assured that Simple Pleasures will be getting some publicity shout outs!

They were surprised when I had my special Masseur come in and give them full body massages. My house special, the "St. Louis Swiss Mocha Mud Bath" is a favorite amongst the clients. Maurice is very good at his job. That boy is *my* relief on my bad days and my secret weapon against a breakdown. Whether it is pedicures, manicures, or the massages the boy is a total wonder. Too bad, he is gay; I would love to go for a ride.

I'm so tired right about now all I want to do is rest for days on top of days. This had been a very eventful but most memorable day. Rachel will be so happy to see the stuff that I got from the promo teams. I was even able to get photos with the women one on one and as a whole group. I will add those to my wall of fame. Rachel will be ecstatic to see the backstage passes we got to the concert as well. I guess I can call home to inform them that I am on the way home.

"Lance, it's Desirae, I'll be home in about thirty to forty minutes. I hope you will be ready to talk when I arrive; I am running late, but I will tell you about the day here at the salon. Lance, are you there?" I hear nothing but total silence, which only brings me back to the thought of our fucked up morning.

"I hear you loud and clear Rae! What happened to you coming home so we could discuss the issues we have before us? You seem not to care about *getting me straight*. I thought you wanted to talk things out! Why are you leaving the salon so late anyways?" He sounded more jealous than disappointed.

"Did you send Rachel off, so we could discuss things in private?"
"Rae, you never cease to amaze me. You were so busy going off on me this morning that you never allowed me to finish telling you the plans for the weekend. Do you know what tomorrow is?"
"What Lance, what is tomorrow?" I asked trying not to sound so irritated.
"It's Rachel's' trip to Chicago with your sister! Damn I can't believe you forgot!"
I am banging my hand into my head now, because I did forget! I cannot let him know that though.

"Lance I did not forget. I already packed her bags, purchased her some new outfits for the trip, plus I left her a pre-paid debit card with about two thousand dollars loaded on it, in her handbag for spending money, along with her expense book! I only wanted you to send her away tonight, so we could talk! How dare you accuse me of forgetting something like that?"

"I know you forgot because she is over your sisters' house now for the slumber party with her cousins and friends that YOU were suppose to be helping your sister chaperone! WHAT NOW DESIRAE?"
Like Orange Juice Jones said in his song, "Walking in the Rain": "COLD BUSTED!" I am going to kill my sis for not reminding me of the sleepover tonight! Why in the hell did I not put that in my blackberry?

"Lance I did forget about the party, but not the trip. I had last minute appointments for Janet and Beyonce! They are here for the weekend concert, and I tell you what: it was crazy but we all were able to handle things. I got pictures, t-shirts and backstage passes for everyone."

I guess I will have to give Rachel's ticket away because she never missed the annual shopping trip to Chicago with her Aunt. They have been doing this for years. It gives me time to unwind, get my house in order and chill out.

"I'm on my way home now, are you still up for talking or what? I can be there real soon."

"No! I am on my way out of town for a meeting and I will not be back until Monday evening. Since you had no sense, nor desire to come home at a reasonable time, I made other plans. Go see Rachel before she leaves. You really need to talk with her and get up to speed, on all the current events. Get things between you and your child right. Help your sister out with what you promised as well.

Desirae, I will only say this to you one more time, so listen, take it to heart, and work on making things happen. I need you, and Rachel needs you. You belong to this family, not that salon or anyone else. Think about what is important. Once you have done that let me know! I am almost to the point of no return. I cannot deal with the lonely nights at home, our daughter missing her mother, and you not being at my side when I need you. I think I have been very understanding. Your moods are changing about as much as I change the channels on the television, when I am surfing for something to watch. Your attitude is almost impossible to deal with. I am here for you, but if you do not want this marriage then neither do I. I'll see you when I return into town!"

"Hello?"

Oh, please tell me this Negro did not hang up in my ear! Okay what is really going on? What does he want me to do? Okay, I guess I will close all my salons, stay at home take care of Rachel, become a soccer mom (what the fuck is that anyways?) and depend on his income alone. I don't think so! I was there for him, I allowed him to establish his business first. It was I, who was hosting all those parties looking like the model wifey and doing all that "community shit" just to make *him* look good. I was starting to think that maybe I needed to increase his pussy allowance! I admit I really have not been too involved with giving Lance some. Only every now and then, or when the thought crossed my mind. Hell, now that I really think about it, he has not been too quick to offer the dick up either.

I guess now since I am doing my thing and I am on top, he wants me to quit. There is no way I will ever do that. Quitting is not in my blood; trust me, I had it tested. Men are always looking for a flunkey to stay at home and do all the *hard work*. He wants laundry done, dinner prepared, our child tended to, house cleaned, *and* a fantastic, mind blowing, coma inducing blowjob all by bedtime. What fucking wonderland is he living in?

I'm just as busy; he should be willing to split these duties in half with me, and then we can sixty-nine each other until we fall asleep. I have labored, done this all before on my own, and I'm tired. I simply cannot take care of home and my career. Shit, nannies and housekeepers, save the day! I am sure that most stars have house cleaners, and nannies helping them out at home. I simply believe Mr. Lance has more going on than what he says is going on, and I will find out!

True, marriage is all about sacrifice, but one thing remains the same. You are born as an individual and you will die as an individual. Never sacrifice your own self-happiness for the happiness of others. When it's all said and done...you, the individual must be happy. Life is for the living...not the dead! I gotta do what makes me happy. I'm following my dreams!

Chapter 6:
Caution on the Road Ahead!

I couldn't get to my sister's house fast enough to see my child and spend some time with her. I know we have been drifting apart, but I love my baby. Rachel means the world to me. I really wanted to talk to Lance earlier in the day, but I had clients to serve, my shop needed to be introduced to some new world order; and to be truthful...I really don't know how to look my husband in his eyes with another man on my mind.

Damn, getting into Denise's house was like trying to attain clearance into a military base. This girl lives all the way out in West County and she locks her house up as tight as a maximum-security prison.
I knock and my knocks go unanswered, so I use my key to get in.

"Hey sis, finally glad you could make it! These kids are driving me nuts. How was the salon today; did any one famous stroll through?" Niecy questioned as she was placing her groceries in her double wide walk-in pantry.

My sister is crazy; she loves to hear about my days at the salon, including the repair stories. I cannot seem to understand why people are always trying to do their own hair! That shit needs outlawing in all states! People should leave the hairstyling to the professionals. They should consider it their *'I love me, time'.*

"Sis, where is Rachel, I need some time with my baby."

"She is upstairs with Deanna, picking out outfits, and watching T.V." She responds as she slams a bag of French fries, hot dogs and a few cases of Pepsi on the counter.

"Great, I'll be back down to tell you about Miss Janet and Miss Beyonce!" I teased.

"Oh, hells to the double NO!" She stood up rolling her neck and snapping her fingers. This girl is so animated. Momma said she watched too many cartoons.

"No you did not have my two favorite artists in the house and not call me! Damn Rae, I could have come on in to rub their feet, pull out rollers, or help run bath water! Damn, why you always leaving yo sister out!"

"Cause I know you!" I yelled, while she looked all confused and crazy while shaking here head in denial.

"Know me how? What the hell would I have done Rae-Rae?"

"Your ass would have been trying to form a soul train line, start doing some old ass played out dance move like the 'George Jefferson', trying to get folks to karaoke, and God knows what else. I'll talk to you when I come back down stairs."

"Auntie Rae-Rae is here...Yeah!" My niece roared out in such excitement as she jumps up and down on her Bratz canopy bed.

"Hey Rachel, momma needs to talk to you for a minute." No response, she doesn't even look my way. Okay, looks like Rachel and I need to have some mother daughter time.

"Deanna, why don't you go on downstairs and help your mother with making the snacks."

"Okay, auntie." She looks at Rachel and puts her mouth over her lips as if there was some oath of secrecy between both of them. I try not to give into the fact that I have caught on to their act.

"Rachel sweetheart, is there something that you would like to talk about?" I tried to read her body language to see if she was upset, shy, confused or embarrassed; but I could not make out anything.

"Okay, then I will talk. I know I have been extremely busy with the salon, the community projects and everything; but I just want to say I am sorry. I know I have missed the recitals, games and our 'special days' together without dad, but please don't hate me." I am begging now because I see the tears building up in my baby's eyes and all I can do is cry for her.

"Momma, I know you be busy and you do the best you can do all the time. This is nothing new for you momma, so I am used to it. It's really daddy I been upset at, but I've been blaming you only to make him think that I'm not onto his games!"

At this moment, all someone had to do was take a picture of my face, develop it and tear it into a million pieces, because my look was very puzzled! The niceness starts to fade away, the impatience sets in but I keep my cool because I want to hear what she has to say.

"Rachel, tell me what you *think* is going on baby!"

"Momma, daddy is cheating on YOU!"

"Rachel, are you sure you just didn't see daddy with a client, or talking to a friend, or handling business over the phone?" I asked trying not to sound surprised, pissed and curious all at the same time. *Who is his raggedy dick out humping?*

"Momma I am not a baby, I'm ten years old!"

"Nine." I reminded her.

"Okay nine and a half." She hints, giving me a reminder that her birthday is close.

I know what you grown folks be talking about *and* doing. I was in daddy's room hiding in the closet waiting to jump out and scare him, and that's when I heard it."

"What is *it* Rachel?"

"That dirty phone call!" She said, with her head lowered, and trying her hardest to avoid all eye contact with me.

"Baby, hold your head up. You are my child; I do not ever want you to feel afraid, embarrassed, shy, and nervous about *anything* when we talk. We are women, and we can talk about anything. Momma wants you to know everything about these so called men that walk the earth, including the meatless bone they carry in their pants!"

"MOMMA!" she screeched out in embarrassment as she placed her had over her mouth to hide her grin.

"I'm for real baby." I couldn't hold in my laugh, because something told me the tears would not be far behind.

"Momma, he was talking about a weekend get away on the beach would do him just fine. It would give him time to think about if he wanted to be married to the "BITCH DIVA." He said he was longing to feel loved and appreciated before he grew too old and no one cared anymore. Next he was on to saying you better be ready for this big.... you know momma!"

"Spit it all out Rachel, every word and no skipping and leaving shit out!"

"Be ready for his big old DICK! Dang moms, why you make me say it?" she yells as she turns her back towards me.

"Look, how long did the call last and did your dad find you in the closet?" I questioned as I turned her back towards my direction.

"It lasted for about thirty minutes, and probably longer afterwards."

"What baby? Explain yourself Rachel!" I impatiently asked.

"He was getting his work clothes together for his next day of work and he was coming towards the closet, so I laid myself out on the floor, and played sleep. When he opened the closet, he said he had just found the most precious thing in his entire world passed out on the floor sleep, to that HOOKER on the phone.

"RACHEL!" I yelled. I could see at this point, she didn't give a damn, because I saw pain smeared all over her face.

"He carried me to my room and tucked me in my bed, and then I could hear him start the conversation back up again. I just cried myself to sleep, and hoped you would walk in and get a chance to hear him on the phone."

"Okay, you know momma loves you right?" I started to explain as I took my only child into the center of my soul. I held her tightly as I explained *life* to her. "There are some things adults do, that are bad. However, keep in mind that your father and I love you very much. If our marriage ended today, it *WILL NOT* alter the love we have for you. Do not worry, I will find out what is going on, but keep your cool, and stop being upset with me! Rachel, our relationship is great and will be even better.

Mommy will be making many changes in the near future, but daddy does not need to know anything we talked about tonight! You understand?"

"It's all good moms. Glad I was able to see you before we all went out of town."

Enjoy your trip with your auntie, and please try not to buy stuff you don't need!"

We both laugh out and voiced out in unison as we snapped our fingers in the air imitating the Ant wan Merewether character from the show; "In Living Color".

"We don't need it now, but we will need it later, SO GET IT GIRL!" we giggled together like two crazed little girls.

"Okay silly girl, gone head and get downstairs and enjoy your friends and cousins. I'm going to talk to your auntie, and get ready for my long day tomorrow. Oh yeah, Beyonce and Janet came by the shop tonight and we hooked them up from head to toe!"

"What? Momma, I would kill to see them in person. I would have loved to meet them!" she whined, as she appeared to be in a star daze.

"Sweetie, you were all the way here with auntie and it was kind of last minute, but don't worry I got you plenty of pictures, and other stuff. It will be in your room when you get back."

"You're, the bomb momma! I love you."

"Love you too baby."

My sister and I talked about the turn of events, while knocking off those hot dogs, fries and those Pepsi's. We swore to hold and uplift each other in life no matter what!" She was really pissed about the whole ordeal of Lance and his mystery call. What came next was a question that even I could not answer.

"Rae-Rae you think he is aware of your 'outside' activities?"

"Damn, Denise why you got to go there?"

"Why not go there, Rae? You need to be careful out there. I just want to know why you're still married to him."

"Look if I wasn't married and still out here doing what I do, what would you have to say to me?"

"Be careful out there Rae-Rae."

"Exactly, so why does he matter? If you so mad at him, why you care if he knows?"

"You are so selfish at times. Do you know these bastards will kill you now and days for doing the shit you doing? I mean its ok for *them* to fuck around, but something makes them go off; click and sometimes they never come back! Do you want Rachel to deal with that shit for life? Her mother dead and her father sent off to prison. Hell, next I may have to put in her a nuthouse!" she screams out. I grab her hand to alert her that she needs to calm down.

"Sis there is so much shit you don't even know about. If I told you, would think different about your sister! However, I will say that most of my problems are self-inflicted and that is where I am ending with this topic! I'm trying to make them all fade to darkness Denise, I really am. Regarding Lance, I will find out what is going on. Please don't worry; you know your sis can handle herself!"

"Rae-Rae, make a promise to me that you won't do some stupid shit!"

"You know I do not make promises, but I'll stand on my word that no one will lose their life in all this bullshit going on. Keep your ears open, your mind sharp and call me if you notice anything out of line. I got shit to do."

We hugged each other as if it was the last time we were ever going to see one another. I love my sister, and she loves me. I am so happy to see her doing well in life and living a stress free. Her husband loves her, she loves him back and their life is complete. She is the one that is blessed. Their life not only looks good to other folks, but it reflects the same thing when they are inside their home! Fuck Master Card, because their love is priceless.

The drive home was a long one, simply because when my thoughts are deep, I tend to slow down and focus more on the mental shit than the road. I finally arrive to my home, and I feel drenched in sadness. My guilt only makes me feel more wet and cold; but then anger appears. I heat up, but shortly thereafter, I dry off with reason.

Love sucks! It is like getting a new puppy. It's all-good in the start, you take care of it, you show it all the attention in the world, you let it sleep with you, and you take it everywhere it can go with you. Then one day the extra playtime, the long walks, and all the little extras stop. The oldness sets in and now you do not want it anymore. How can you keep love alive, when it is lost along the way? FUCK!

Londa B.

I drop my keys on my 'whatever fucking century it was made in' table in my foyer; shouted out commands to turn on the stereo, and the televisions. I guess I am so used to the noise at the salon; that if it's quite for too long, I start doing something bad, like thinking!

From one room to the next the lights come as I make entry into each room. I check to make sure nothing is out of place, or smells different. I never felt like I had to be so 'on guard' in my own house. I hope that motherfucker never decides to bring a bitch up in my house! I got the bail money reserved and the lawyer on speed dial! I check the mountainous pile of mail on the kitchen counter. Nothing is out of the ordinary. New credit card applications, a few bills and more junk mail came today. One piece of mail instantly gets my heart rate going. "THE PHONE BILL IS HERE!" I rip it open and I quickly start analyzing the bill. Most of the numbers I see are ones I know, my parents, his office, the salons, and his side of the family. Why does the New York salon phone number keep showing up is a big question to me? The calls happen to be occurring only at times when I am not at home. What the fuck is going on?

I kept my cool and I decide to run some warm bath water, throw in a couple of bath salt balls, grab myself a bottle of wine, and release my tensions another way.

I throw on my John Legend "*Get Lifted*" CD. This is the CD that makes me take notice of the things around me, and realize that no matter how fucked up things may be in life, all will be all right again in due time. Depending on what song is, playing it makes me feel a certain way, but mostly it inspires me. Okay, it makes me horny as hell too.

What a way to end the day! I think about my daughter, my asshole husband as well as myself. I try to figure out if just leaving Lance would solve my problems, or would things only get worse for me. I feel like I need my family, but I also need my air to be me. To vent, cry, laugh, and even be depressed at times with out having anyone to answer to, or go *discuss* my issues with was a thought that was all too inviting. Then reality slapped the shit out of me.

This world is cold, selfish, and it has no love for no one. People see you up one day and pray for you dead the next. My sister was right, there are many diseases out here, and people are crazy these days. I cannot put Rachel through any unnecessary pain. I knew that bitch *life* already had some in store for my baby, the older she gets.

My own life had too much pain, and I refuse to allow any to come into hers as long as I possibly can.

The night had a lot to offer if you believed in love, and happiness like Al Green once did. That's until those hot grits found his ass. Feeling renewed from my bath, I peered out of my bay window. I started to reminisce into a time and moment in my life, where my heart felt everything in its beat of life. The fall breeze snatches my gown open and my body felt the kisses of the refreshing wind blown autumn breezes. I see my silhouette in the window of my carriage house and I am quite pleased with my 'genetic makeup.' Suddenly a mixture of feelings ranging from excitement, sadness, love, and even fear settle into my spirit. Talk about an emotional roller coaster! I gather my gown to cover myself, hoping that maybe I can cover up these feelings as well.

Now, this old heart is on ice, and the desire for it to convert back to its normal rhythm becomes weaker by the minute only because I realize that I am to blame for my sadness and grief. I should have never allowed ***it*** to happen.

"It is what it is!" That is what I have taught myself to say for years, and now I believe it. How can you change something that is going to happen anyways?

Have I ever really been able to love a man for who he really is, and not what I desire for him to be? Damn, this is my (okay, most women's) problem. My own soul's desires have gotten me into a lot of trouble. I liked Lance from the moment I saw him, but then what. What made me latch on to him? What has kept me here for all of these years? I have heard people talk about being in love and all the crazy shit it makes you do, but to be truthful...either I was already crazy; or doing crazy shit was not on my menu like the garlic butter rolls at Red Lobster. Maybe the love was never there. Maybe it was all about being convenient, and a perfect opportunity. Who am I kidding? I know that *is* the reason why!

Maybe all of my answers would come to my mind when I see Lance once he got back, so with that in mind, I did something I had not done in along time, and I know I need my ass kicked for not doing this on a daily basis! It's time to PRAY!

"Lord, please open your arms and pour down on me, a rain shower of forgiveness. For all the missed Sundays at church, the missed acknowledgements of my sins and daily words of praise for you allowing me to live a life of good fortune. I thank you Lord for allowing my child to be healthy, smart and beautiful. Thank you, for holding my family together by not

allowing evil to have a face to present itself in my families' life. I am not a great person, and I am asking you to make everything all right. Lord I need you to work on my mind and my body. I need the will to walk in a righteous manner, and to be more obedient in my marriage –okay Lord you take over from here, not really sure if it's what I want- vows. I need your help, for I know not what to do. I can't pretend that my heart is not skipping and missing the beats of true love, Lord. With these and all other things that I ask in your name oh Lord, let it be. Amen."

Silence and peace is present in the room. My chest lightens and I feel fine. This is the first time in a long while, where I have laid in my own bed and not felt one bit of tension. I know a good nights rest is soon on the way.

"Damn!" I hate it when Lance sets that alarm clock loud like that! I know he did that on purpose before he left. I roll over and slap the hell out of the alarm clock, and I shove myself all the way back underneath the covers. The aroma of my Victoria Secret Vanilla Bean body rub is alerting my hormones and caressing my senses. My nipples are true to the form of pure erectness; my pussy can't even tighten up enough to hold in my sweet juices. Continuous drips of my lusciousness, rolls down the folds of my lips and onto my silk Christian Dior sheets.

I roll over onto my body pillow and grind against it while I stare at my bare body in the mirror that stretches along my entire bedroom wall. *Whoever thought humping a pillow would look so sexy?* I'm so good at getting my self off; I have no need for toys. I love to watch myself when I *love* me. I propped myself up on my triple goose feathered pillows, spread my thighs, and a sea of warm wetness appears. *How sexy is this?* My nipples are dark and true-to-true form. My hips stick out jut far enough to make any brother want to hold on while he pushes all his love deep down inside my walls. My skin looks like pure honey with a kiss of golden rays from the suns beam. I stare directly at myself while licking my full bodied and luscious lips. I pull my *'violin act'* once again. Stringing my clit, like no other. That feeling along with the silk sheets caressing my ass is enough to set me off.

"Oh yes, um, um, um, whoa!" I shout out as I slide down my mountain of pillows!

I need to get my hands insured, because if they ever got hurt... I would be missing many concerts; and the symphonies of self-satisfaction will no longer be playing.

~Chapter 7~

Party Time

Saturday was a day of curiosity and I tell you it didn't kill this kitty cat! When I made it in to the shop, everyone was there, except for two people. The hood city chicks had left! All of their equipment was gone and to my surprise, everything in the store stood accounted for. Thank the Lord. No more time spent wondering when Dae-Dae and Pookie would arrive to my salon to pick up their chickens. I guess they assumed I was firing them today, so they saved themselves the embarrassment. What I did find that was more surprising than the hood rat chicks leaving was a beautiful arrangement of flowers on my desk.

I closed the door, and ran over to the flowers. I opened the card and began to read the funny looking handwriting.

"I hope my therapy is helping you, please make sure you come on Monday for it will help you out tremendously."

I smiled because I knew it was not Lance just by the handwriting alone. What is the good doctor up to? I am trying to read between the lines, but all I get is space!

"Lila, please come into my office when you get a second please." After I overhead paged her, my cell phone rang.

"Hello?" I answered trying to figure out who was calling me from a New York area code.

"Rae, it's me... Lance. Look I will be home in a week. I ran into an old friend of mine, and he talked me into going to this seminar teaching us how to build on our real estate investments, and other real estate stuff. I promise to call you and Rachel daily, and I will let you know when my arrival will be. Is this okay with you?"

"How the hell you gone call me, tell me what you gone do, then ask me if the shit is okay?" Damn he has to be out of his mind!

"*You* were the one that made the speech, talked the talk, and expressed how you felt. I was ready to give this marriage a second looking *(why am I lying?)* at until you called me with this lie. Nevertheless, please don't let your conscious spoil your fun. *Do what makes you happy because I want you to feel all the love and appreciation before you and your big dick get too old to stand!* Please enjoy the week, and I'll enjoy mine. Lance, don't insult me and think that I always have to much on my plate to where I can never look up to see what the hell I'm being served!"

"Rae, I'm coming home today. I don't want to fight, and I don't want to be with out you."

"Save it baby" trying not to sound upset, I start laughing to keep from crying because I feel this shit is so close to being over, like the heat from the pressing comb on the back of my neck!

"I'm going to the Janet and Beyonce concert, and then I'm flying to Miami to see my cousins. Take your time and make us that good-bye money!"

"Good-bye money?" He asks in a curious tone of voice.

"Lance...our shit is over!"

"I'm done playing and you should be too!" I struck back.

"Wait Rae, what are you saying? This bastard can't take a hint for shit.

"Look, I'm getting ready to enjoy my weekend then, I'm off to Miami. I guess we should be meeting right up at the airport when we get home.

We'll talk then. Be safe in your travels, and I promise to be civil about everything."

"You're a smart ass Rae! That *new* doctor isn't helping you out too much."

"Keep thinking that Lance, I'm getting better each time I go. I can ***feel*** it! The drugs he is giving me are good for my *nerves*! I'll be okay, you'll see." I hissed out to him while rolling my eyes towards the sky as if Ray was right there sucking my pussy at my desk while I spat out my last words to Lance.

Okay I got the concert tonight, and then from there I can take a plane out of town. From there…it is my time to grind! I love hanging out with my cousins. Las Vegas is not the only place where the skeletons lay.

Lila finally makes her way into the office.

"As you know those chicken heads quit. I'll be out of town this weekend, so if you need me just call me on my cell phone, Okay.

"No problem Rae. You cool?"

"Yeah girl, just gone take some time to chill with the family in Miami, then I will come on back home. Hey, thanks for helping me out last night with our special guests. I do apologize for being hard with you as well."

"It's all its business I know how it goes. Enjoy your weekend Rae."

"See you on Tuesday." We ended the day with a sister hug and plenty of apologies.

Damn this concert is the bomb! I really need to leave so I can get a head start to Miami though! There is so much commotion going on backstage it is unreal! Folks changing backstage in the middle of everywhere, peeps mingling and getting their freak on as well. I can't believe some of the shit that goes down on these tours and at these after parties. I thought my shit was wild, but my momma said; "There will always be someone finer than you, richer, and most certainly; a better fuck!" I always laugh when I think of that shit, because everything she has told me has come to past!

"Enjoying the concert Miss Lady?" A real
Deep and velvet voice echoed into my ear.

I turned around to see who in the hell has snuck up behind me so quickly.

"Yes, I am!" I yelled trying to make sure, he heard me, but something tells me that my body language will be the speakers. *Damn is this brother on the market or what?*

"You came to the concert alone?"

"Yes, why do you ask?" I asked, while trying not to be too obvious as I checked out his dick compartment. Damn he's fine! Nothing is sexier than a tall assed, dark skinned brother with a bald fade haircut. Darkness is a mystery that I try reading all the time!

"I just figure that this is a concert with two of the sexiest entertainers, who would come solo? The sound alone will get a couple grinding and pulsating to these sexy tunes. Next thing you know, the two of you will be having brain damaging sex!"

Okay, this brother is most certainly advertising that he's interested into having some next level sex. I'm tempted because no man has ever threatened me with the idea of fucking until I am retarded! I'll leave this concert with a fucking football helmet on!

I instantly walk over towards him to see if his scent is there. Yup, I'm like a dog. The scent of sex, lust and some good assed cologne has to present for me to fuck. Damn, his scent is exotic. One I can't quite pin down and I *know* my colognes.

"You like?"

"I think I can!" I reply with my she-devil grin as I stand only a few inches from his solid frame.

He grabs my breasts and then presses his solid frame against my small body onto the speakers behind us. The beat pulsating into my back sent my body (including my pussy) into full throttle.

"Pull them panties off!" he commands

"Right here, now?"

"Come on and get ready to get your back blasted full of vibrating beats, while I pound some tunes down into that pussy of yours. It's so wet I can smell it in the air tonight!"

"I…I…" damn I sound like the re-mix to Joe's song 'Stutter' or is this one of those signs early stage retardation.

He instantly drops to his knees and his head goes underneath my dress. I couldn't decide which part of my body would spread wider, my legs or my mouth! He was smacking, licking and sucking as if he was trying to suck all the crabmeat out of a shell! I kept looking around to see who saw him feasting upon me, but we hid behind the huge speakers.

Fuck, for the few who did saw us, they let us be. I couldn't give a damn who was around at this point 'DL' is about to throw her own damn concert.

"You like them long, hard and fat, don't you?" he asked as he rose from my nesting place with my juices all over his lips. Here touch my man! He got something for you baby!"

"DAMN!" I yelled while backing up!

"Baby, that's a trip to the Gyn's office!" I replied, while feeling what he was working with. I mean my hand couldn't even wrap all the way around it. I had to hold it as if I was about to eat a burrito!

"Not if you know how to ride it baby!"

He was pushing all that rock up against me and my pussy must have sensed it near by because the bitch started throbbing so bad, that I just had to give in!

"Pull it out daddy, so I can spread some of this good juice on ya!"

"Ooh," I slowly moaned as he shoved all of his nine something inches in me. It was fat and it had a fucking pulse! *What in the hell is happening? OH my Lord, I am going retarded. I had better not start drooling!* I can feel the veins, the ridges and every crevice that is on his dick as he slides in and out. This is some extreme shit. I've never gotten this lose and wild in all of my natural life. One would think I was high ***and*** full of hypnotic. This has always been something I fantasized about, but now—today, here.

"Yeah, take it like a good girl. Your pussy is out of sight wet. I want to eat some more of that!"

"No please, harder! Fuck me until we blow these damn speakers out!"

"Okay, you got it!" he exclaimed.

From there, it was on. With all his ridges pressing against my girls' lips, my walls and my clit, it felt like my insides had sprung a leak. The juices began to flow. I closed my eyes and suddenly felt them rolling into the back of my head. I leaned back on him as if I was going to pass, out. From there he grabbed my nipples and started pulling on them so hard and fierce as if he were doing a strengthening exercise.

"UUUMMM, you feel so good! I can't hold back, please harder, harder, harder." I moaned while rejoicing for getting some of his good dick!

"Devin made that pussy come huh?" he whispered.

"Take this king into your mouth and swallow hard!"

To my knees I went. I was face to face with the king of them all. As I said, it was fat, thick, hard and very fucking round. I swallowed it whole, like the good girl I am! *Damn Miss Thang, pat yourself on the back when you done for sucking this monster!* I swore he was thrusting his shit in and out so hard; I had to hold onto his strong, muscular thighs just to keep me from flying across the back stage with each thrust! I just knew there was going to be a hickey in the back of my fucking head!

"Oh, shit, here it come girl, get ready to swallow!"

I felt this huge man buckle but then he quickly regained his position. From there I felt a flood occur in my mouth.

Oh Lord, this dude could shoot some shit out!

"You give a good ride baby." He said as he gently wiped his juices from my lip.

"You said your name was Devin, huh?"

"Yes. What is yours?"

"Rae."

"Is that it?"

"That's all for now."

I can't believe I am even going there with this dude. I'm trying to stay on my new path to being a better woman and I end up banging it out with his fine ass at the biggest concert of the year. Way to go girl, three bumps and a pump for Rae-Rae!

"Look, give me your card and I'll contact you once I get back in from Miami. I have some business to handle, but I'll be happy if we could hook up once I got back into town."

"Oh, you're a cold woman."

"Excuse me?"

"You mean to tell me, that you just gone up and leave, then promise to holla at me later? I was hoping..."

"Look baby, I don't know what you were hoping, but you couldn't have hoped for much cause I know you saw this five carat ring on the *"ISE MARRIED"* finger!" I yelled, while still scrambling around trying to gather myself.

"Damn, I couldn't see shit the way I was down under."

"Look Devin, you most certainly know how to work a sister over, but what else you got to offer?"

"Okay, I'll wait on you. I see you on some next level type of shit. I'll give you my answer once your return from Miami."

"Thanks for understanding."

"I hope you plan to make some time for me, here and there. I would most certainly love to take some time to get to know you. When I saw you, something hit me."

"What...your dick?" I joked

"Okay, you got some jokes."

"No, your vibe and essence is too much not to be noticed. You're like a breath of freshness. I want to be revived everyday by those juicy lips. Just make some time for me; no bullshit, no problems, I promise. I'm not crazy; I have no kids, no ex's and a fat..."

"Yes, the dick I know!"

"No, see you're too smart for your own damn good Miss Lady."

"A fat bank account, which allows me to spend all the time in the world loving and pleasuring my lady!" Look, don't make me beg ya; make sure you put some time to the side for me sweetness." He begs while squeezing my ass.

"What the fuck does the money have to do with it?" I asked while shifting away from him.

"Money is international! It's something the entire world needs and wants. Everything else is seconds, thirds and so forth. In addition, you're high class. I know you aren't looking for all the love in the world from a broke dick, ugly assed brother!"

"Hells, naw! Now *YOU* got jokes."

I gently grabbed his hand hoping that an act of sincerity would show him that I am honest about what I am saying, so I could get the fuck on my way.

"Look I promise to call you."

"See you soon Miss Lady" as he gently kissed the back of my neck.

Damn, I am kind of feeling old boy. Maybe I can place him on my goodies shelf as a good standby, when all the others are pissing me off. Oh, that's right...I am trying to be good. I got too much shit going on right now, to think about some man that just nearly fucked me into the first stage of retarded ness.

Chapter 8:
Party Over

T*O the left, to the left*... okay, I'll stop with *"Irreplaceable"* song for now. I'm feeling good and hell yeah, that Devin has the entire world to do with it. When your mind speaks, you must listen to it. I was glad I packed my bags and gathered my shit together before going to the shop and running my usual marathon of Saturday errands. The chicken-headed sisters' leaving was truly a blessing. Every one else is safe for now, unless they decide that they can do better. This night has been one to remember. Hell, the start to this whole weekend is one I can't forget. I guess I better make this trip to Miami a good one; cause I know the real drama will start once I get back home. I'm so glad I left the concert early. I usually try to stay in its entirety, so I can hang out with the stars and viciously get my 'after party' on. FUCK! Does the phone have to ring every time I get inside my car?

"Hello?"

Click!

Who the hell, just called me and hung up? Just as I am checking my caller Id, my phone starts to ring out of control.

"Hello?"

"Rae, it's me Lance. Don't hang up! I know you are mad at me, but please listen to me-"

"Baby look I can't talk now, it's raining badly and I am trying to drive. I'll call you soon as I get to Miami with my family!"

CLICK!

Okay, I shifted my thought back to the original call. What a surprise, there was a number that showed up on my caller ID that should have never popped up. Who's calling me from *my* New York salon on a Saturday night? I know damn well they're never open late on weekend nights. I can't help but to think that someone who has no business being in my salon is doing more than getting a wash and set! With that thought- - "New York, here I come!"

I pressed the pedal to the floorboard of my ride and visions of a take off were in clear view!

I know I looked like a lunatic parading and short cutting through the airport like a star that was trying to lose the paparazzi. Damn, trying to reach the ticket counter is like running upwards on an escalator going down!

"One, one way ticket to New York City, and make it the next flight out." I said, while trying to catch my breath.

Knowing my damn luck, I'll have to wait on the next plane, which will not be boarding for several hours.

"Okay, what class?" the clerk asks.

"Baby it doesn't matter if you give me a fucking flying magic carpet; I'll take whatever you have and be *very* grateful."

"I got you covered! I have a one-way ticket for my tired and panicked sista! For the price of $234.59, you can be on your way. The flight leaves gate G-17 in thirty-five minutes. There are no layovers! This flight is a direct flight!" The sweet clerk stated.

"Thank you, honey." I said while slipping the young woman my credit card.

I immediately called my girl, Wanda in New York. I was hoping she would be able to help me out with a few things once I got to the 'Big Apple.'

"Wanda?"

"Rae?"

"Hey girl, what's going on?" I asked.

"Not much, you in town?"

"Almost there. What you got planned?"

"Chillin out and laying on my ass the entire weekend. You should fly on over. I haven't seen you in a while. You know the last time you were here, you completely played a sister!"

"Okay, forgive me on that. It's hard to sight see, visit old friends *and* take care of business. If I don't stick to my plans once I get to the city…I can kiss my plans of conducting business bye-bye!"

"Rae, please don't make me feel guilty for wanting to spend time with my best friend."

"I won't. Hey, look Wanda. I need you to pick me up at the airport in about two hours. I need someone to drive me around on a few errands and then I figure we can go take a bite out of the Big Apple. I know that damn city of yours never sleeps."

"Sure, it's not a problem at all. Rae, you sound a little distant. Where is your mind at girl?"

"I got a few things I need to handle; I'll fill you in once I get to New York. I prefer to talk face to face."

"Whatever you need I got your back. God knows, you have been there so many times for my ass."

"Okay, I'll call once I land."

"See you soon girl."

It's good to have friends all over the world. Shit you never know when you gone need them. I never make a habit of allowing too many people to know anything about my personal life. Few folks I can trust. I've been hurt and I had to learn about shit the hard way! Hmm, speaking of the hard way let me call Ray.

"Hello, you've reached the office of..."

Damn, he always answers my calls. It's late, so it's not as if he is seeing patients or something. Why isn't he picking up? Hell, maybe he's tired and just need to get some rest since I laid it on him earlier today!

Oh well, I will most certainly be in need of is services once I return home. I'm sure he has something special planned for me since he is requesting my whole day be set-aside for him.

"Wanda, I'm here. Where did you park? I'm in such a hurry!" For some reason, ever since I felt the plane making its landing my heart rate has not reached its resting state. I want this shit to be over like football season!

"Rae! Here I am. Look to the left girl!"

Trying to blow my hair out of my face, I finally come into clear view of my girl.

"Wanda!"

We ran to each other and hugged until we noticed all the folks staring at us as if we were crazy or something. They got their nerves!

"Okay, fuck waiting to get to the car. Spill the fucking beans bitch! I mean the whole damn can too and don't forget to scrape out the ones that didn't come out on their own!"

I love this girl. We go back a few million miles. When I started my salon in New York, she was my first customer. We instantly took a liking to one another. The best part about her is that she was so REAL and down to earth! I never felt jealousy, or the need to compete from her. It didn't matter what went down she had my back. Beauty must be her middle name. Wanda was about five feet, eleven and had the body of an African Queen. Her voice was heavy with assertiveness, and her hazel eyes painted the picture she wanted you to see. Her beautiful long black hair had streaks of gold that high lighted her toasted, golden honey skin. Girl friend was together in every aspect.

From the start of my business, she had no problem making sure that all of New York knew about Simple Pleasures. Not to mention the fact that she is an outstanding marketing and advertising rep for one of the biggest Ad Agencies in the NYC. Girlfriend knew plenty of folks and she just has a way of working on people.

"Girl, I think Lance is here cheating on me. He called me while I was in St. Louis on the way to the airport. He fucked up cause guess where he called me from?"

"Where, Rae?"

"My New York salon, that's where!"

I cried while drawing my fingers into a binding cringe.

She gasped as if I told her I was pregnant with triplets.

"Yes he did. He hung up; once he figured out that I was gone pick his ass up, by checking my caller-id. He was too stupid to call me from the cell phone on the first call!"

"What a dumb-ass!"

"Now you know where we going and how quick we need to get there, right?"

"Baby the wheels on my Benz are smoking already!"

"Let's ride!" I yelled as we started running out of the airport.

The music is fiercely booming from the speakers as we sped to the salon. The sky had no need for the moon, because the city lights did a great job of highlighting the Big Apple's skyline. Damn, I love New York. It's the only city in the world, which can still stand tall, with all the shit it has going on it! The city lights my soul with excitement.

The thought of me whipping Lance's ass for using my salon as some sex palace to fuck his hoe; is a thought that makes me want to upgrade my shit to the next level. I mean I can see me throwing him out now! Beyonce is singing loud as the control volume will allow her too, while I march around my home to the beat of 'Irreplaceable' looking very sexy! Still kicking his shit *'to the left'* while holding my composure in my six-inch Jimmy Choo's and a sexy piece of nothing lingerie. He'll regret this for the rest of his life.

"Turn the music down and cut the car off Wanda!" I yelled while trying to case my own joint to figure out who all is in my salon. *Why in the hell is it so necessary for folks to turn the radio down when trying to find an address? I never understood that, but now I see my own self-doing it. How funny.* I see three cars and they're all rental cars. What is going on?

I turned to my friend and I prepared to give her 'that talk' that's simply a warning that some CLASS A- CLASSIFIED shit is about to go down. I guess this is our version of "Training Day" where I tell her ass to woman on up, or get out before the flames arise!

"Look, you have been there for me as long as I can remember as well. I do not want you to put anything in jeopardy. Whatever happens I take the blame. You knew nothing! Do you understand me? I am giving you the choice to stay in the car, or to come in with me. The choice is yours."

I could tell that everything I said went in one ear and out the other by the dazed look; she was giving me while popping on some Double Mint gum, like a five-dollar hooker!

"Bitch, when we get done on the inside, we gone talk about you sniffing on that white shit! I know you ***must*** be on crack or something if you think I'm gone let my girl, roll up in there solo! Yo sister said you been tripping!"

"Let's do it!" I said.

At this point, I am so scared to see what is behind my salon doors, but damn...***KARMA IS A MOTHER FUCKER! I had this shit coming long time ago! Woman on up Miss Rae, it is time to deal with reality!***

I opened my salon door and we raced to the alarm system. I quickly noticed that the system wasn't even on. Wanda and I crept around in pure silence trying to piece shit together!

"Rae! Come look at this shit!" Wanda blurted out

"What the fuck?" I shouted, and then I quickly placed my hand over my mouth, trying to mute my awful screech.

"Rose petals from the door area to the spa area?" Wanda quizzes.

"Let's follow it." I eagerly suggested.

As we follow the petals, the sound of music becomes clearer. I'm almost tempted to sing along, until I heard what the fuck was playing. This punk motherfucker has the nerve to be playing our favorite (Raheem DeVaughn's, *"Believe")* song while he is pleasuring some hoe! I can't wait to bust in on this fucking party! Like Orange Juice Jones said… "Cold Busted!"

The closer we got to the room the combined fusion of my expensive body oils and bath salts accented the very air in which we were breathing. Inhaling the sweet aromas of vanilla one moment and exhaling the essence of lavender the next. The tears were welling up in my eyes and I started to tremble. A part of me wanted to kick the door down and the other part did not want to enter at all. Hell, with all the dirt I had done, we can just call it even. When we got to the door, Wanda grabbed my hand.

"I love you Rae. No matter what is behind this door, it stays right here between you and me. Your shit is safe with me. Promise me you will walk away with your pride! That's what eats the motherfucker up! Not saying shit at all sometimes is the best thing you can do in situations like this! Trust me girl, it makes them mad crazy!"

"You know I don't make promises I can't live on!" I snapped while rolling my eyes and stomping my feet.

"My mind clicks more than the rail counter at the subway station here in New York; don't expect me to go in ready to accept and give out *forgiveness* passes!"

Suddenly we heard a loud moan from a woman. Then I heard Lance's voice.

"You like it from the back, don't you bitch?" Lance questioned.

I instantly place my hand over my mouth, while Wanda hung her head down low, swinging it side to side in pure disbelief.

"Ouch, damn man!" Lance screamed.

"How you like *my* big dick in *your* ass?" the somewhat familiar voice echoed.

"Yeah, I love it dude! Put it on me and do it right! Next time lube it up though man; you tearing a brother up!"

"I knew you could handle this!" the somewhat familiar voice said.

Wanda instantly looks over at me in pure disgust, while imitating herself regurgitating onto my salon floor.

"Rae, what the fuck is going on?" Wanda asks.

I couldn't answer. I was shocked and instantly frozen into position.

"Let's find out!" Wanda shouts and she prepares to break her predatory position.

"Wait. I want to watch! When I walk away, I don't want to leave room for explanations. I want to catch their ass in the middle of their act. I want to see this shit!"

"Rae, you're sick! Its enough they all naked and talking filthy!"

"Naw, I'm just crazy!"

We rose up to the glass level of the door and to our surprise, what we found was nothing we could ever imagine seeing ***(FUCK what happens on the internet and magazines, this shit is crazy all right here in MY***

***salon!*)** in all of our life here on earth and anything thereafter. My heart bout slipped straight out of my ass!

"Lance? Lila? Ray?" I chanted out, repeatedly about three times, hoping that the image before my very own eyes would change. I don't think a genie could change this scene with a million fucking blinks.

"Yeah baby!" Lance shrills out!

"I'm about to let go all over that ass!"

"Yes Lance. I'm about too, also!" Lila squealed like the dirty pig bitch she is.

"Well then, make that three yall, because Daddy Ray needs to spray!" Ray sings out in a very devious tone voice.

"Wanda, get Lila!"

"I got Lance!"

"I'll break this vase over Ray's head before he even has a chance to pull out!"

"Wait, I'll need these as well."

"Rae, I know you're not about to do what I think you gone do!"

"Move in sista!" I commanded.

We busted through the door and executed our plan, like a special military operations unit. I took my vase and cracked it clean over Ray's head. Lance falls over on Lila trying to shield her from the flying ceramic.

"Get over here bitch!" Wanda yelled at Lila while grabbing her by her hair. *What happened to walking out with our pride?*

"Rae, wait!" Lance yells trying to shield his face.

"You like it hot and steamy Lance? Well here, this will serve you just right you mother fucker!" I reached back for my weapon of choice that suited Mr. Lover man just right.

"Rae! Stop! Please do not do it! AWWWW!" he screams like a hot bitch in the middle of summer. *Damn this feels good! I want to burn his ass again.*

I deeply embedded the hot Marcella iron right onto his left bicep.

"Welcome to the---***"I fucked up on my wife"*** FRAT! Hope you like your tattoo! That should hold you for life, you fucking dog!"

"Baby stop, I'm sorry! Please can't we fucking talk?" he begs and screams while slithering around on the floor like a snake without its head!

"Fuck talking! This shit is over. I can't do this shit anymore. I admit I did my shit as well; but Lance...not only did you fucking cut the cake, but you've eaten the whole damn thing on your own!" I yelled while pacing the floor in a crazed manner while swinging my arms all over the place.

"I can't deal with you in my life any more. If I have to think about if I ever loved you, then the answer is just as clear as crystal at our wedding reception! I'll have all your shit shipped to your summer home, don't come by; do not call unless it has to do with talking to Rachel. I'll see you in court!"

"Now say cheese!"

"Say cheese? Bitch what you talking bout?" he asks in that dumb-assed voice I hate.

CLICK~!

"Now your shit is all in this camera! Now I want you to fuck with me." I said as I continued to snap pictures of their dirty and filthy love scene.

I turned around to see Wanda still whipping Lila's ass. I could not help but laugh. Cause my girl was working her well into overtime!

I guess it is time for NINO TO TALK TO G-MONEY!

"Bitch, I can't believe it was you, out of all the people; you had to come along and start fucking my husband? I had others in mind, but you?" I replied, as I snatched the bitch up by her collar. Wanda steps back to take in the view.

"Help me remember what my 'New Jack City' attitude gone do." I joked; reminding her about the so-called sincere talk she called herself having with me in my salon office back in St. Louis.

"Stand up bitch, be a woman! I want to make sure you understand as well as hear every fucking word I have to say!"

"Rae, wait you..."

"Don't talk, ***Mrs. Nino Brown*** is talking now bitch!"

"Don't return to my salon. Don't ever visit or contact anyone at any of my salons. I'll sue the shit out of you and post these pictures all over the web and wherever else, if you leak any of this shit out! Finally, your shit will be delivered by..."

"Fed- Ex, I know." She faintly responds as I tightened up on her hair, which tightly locked around my hand.

"Good girl, glad you know the routine.

"This shit hurts." I said as I pointed to my heart.

"I don't ever want to see you again. What you have done is not about me; it is about you and all the issues you have with your self. I trusted you, we grew up together and most of all...you was my girl! Bitch, I told you to **NEVER** cross the line. It's very apparent that you not only don't give a damn about what I say, but you apparently must think I can't deliver like

'FED-EX' on my promises. Well, you will see how easy it won't be; to get another job, you whore."

With those final words, I reached all the way back to old school and slapped her ass into new school.

"I'm so sorry!" she screamed as she crawled across the floor trying to gather her things.

"Get out bitch!" I roared!

"You're no better and judgment will be taken against you too, Desirae." Lila slowly stuttered out while gathering her things.

"Please, keep it moving before I become compelled to whip your ass for the second time." Damn, momma was right, life showed up and showed out on me today!

Suddenly I turn my attention towards Lance.

"I don't know where your new residence will be, his place or your own, but make sure you send it to me soon. I want to get the divorce going on as soon as possible! I don't want any explanations about anything here. Not tonight anyways!" *I am so glad I do not have a gun right now.*

"Rae, just let me explain." He begs while reaching his burned arm out towards me.

"Explain what? How you like getting fucked in the ass now?" You have totally put some new shit on my therapy…"

"Oh, that's right; I got to find a new therapist now!"

"How did this shit get started?" I questioned, while I pointed over to Ray's body that lay spread eagle across the floor.

While Lance was still holding his left arm, trying to treat the burn marks, he thinks before he responds. I had to take a seat, because all of this shit was wearing me thinner by the minute.

"I'll throw this bitch out, then I'll be right outside the door. Call me if that big punk bitch starts to come to!" Wanda said.

"Get up hoe, party is over!"

"Wait, I got to put my clothes on!" Lila said while she quickly snatched away from Wanda.

"Too late, do all of that shit outside" Wanda replied as she dragged Lila by her hair, while she was kicking and screaming throughout the salon.

I turned back towards Lance and gave him that 'well, spit the truth' look.

"He came after me!"

"You're a fucking liar!"

"He's bi-sexual Rae. I'm sure you had to know."

"Know how Lance? He fucks as if he is the point guard for team P.U.S.S.Y! There was never a reason for me to question his sexuality."

"It seems you know way more than I do. How did you two meet?"

"We met when I took my father on that 'Brothers in Christ Cru sin the Seas' tour about seven months ago."

"What?"

"Yes, he was the featured speaker. He's a minister. You know I had to take dad, he loves events like those."

"Fuck your daddy! He's probably a fag too!" I blurted out in my most hateful tone of voice.

"Look, keep your mouth off of dad!" Lance yells, while taking distance from me on the bench.

"Great! I had an affair with a backsliding gay minister! Get back to the fucking story." I snapped.

"Anyways, when I went to his book signing that's when the conversation started. He went on to say how he had heard from one of the other brothers from St. Louis during our networking social. News was out about me being an excellent agent and that he wanted to retain my services when he relocated to St. Louis. He stated that he wanted to buy a home in the Chesterfield area."

"So you mean to tell me... Wait! What the fuck is up with you? When did *you* decide to start getting butt action?"

"Rae, you can be so cold and uninviting sometimes." Lance said while shaking his head side to side as if he wanted to knock the shit out of me.

"Go head, hit me and get burned again!" I smarted off, while holding my Marcella Irons in my hand.

"Rae, I've been fighting these feelings for a real long time. Momma has had her clues, but for all she knows, I'm happily married and she has a beautiful grand child. I can't have them finding out about this."

"Well it will come; you can bet your sweet, house selling ass on that! I can't believe this shit!" I said, while giving him much attitude.

"I'm glad my parents are both dead, because this shit would have torn them apart- - - literally speaking!" I confessed.

During that moment, my tears welled up. I can't let this snake see me down though. I instantly inhaled my tears, and then I looked at Lance.

"How long have you been fucking other men?"

"Ray was my first...and my last!" Lance said.

"I ought to slap you with a side plate of ***bullshit*** and a whole order of ***asshole please***! You will need the help of Jesus ***and*** his Father to deliver you from the feelings you hold deep down in your heart, groin and asshole! (No, I didn't say that, yes I did!) I know from working around many gays and lesbians that this is not some shit can turn on and off like a water faucet. I've heard their stories and in some ways... I have even felt their heartaches. If you try to turn those feelings off, you gone be even more twisted than Chubby Checker! Whatever team you decide to play for...be real with your shit! What made you do it?"

It took him a minute to respond. Then he glanced over at Ray, while he lay passed out and spread eagle on the floor. Lance finally turns back to face me and in an instant, I could see the love for the same man I wanted to be with all over *my* husbands face.

"I loved the way he made me feel. I felt that if I was going to try "it" out, it had to be with a man like Ray. He is sensitive, caring, understanding, very non-judgmental and very handsome. I thought for a moment that maybe 'my boy' was thinking of you while I was talking to Ray. That feeling died out like a cigarette in an ash trash, when I saw him the second time at the house viewing."

"How so Lance, explain."

"My dick wouldn't go down for shit. I couldn't control my feelings at all! Its kind of like all the shit you said you felt when you were trying to deny me access to visit his office with you, for therapy. Do you remember that? You tried to deny me to something that I had already had! I knew the whole time you were doing him. He told me himself."

SLAP~!

I hope his face is crisp and hard, just like I order my bacon!

I couldn't help but to knock the arrogance and pride right out of his ass.

"Okay, I deserved that; it was a very mean thing to say. I'm sorry Rae." Lance apologized while wiping the blood away from his lip. That rock of mine must have made contact!

"Loving a man like Ray made it all the more easier for me to say yes. I'm sure you felt the same way Rae." Lance said.

"Look, you need to get your life together." I said, while trying to rub the sting out of my hand after delivering a high wattage slap to his face like the electric company.

"Gay, straight or whatever you choose to be; that's a choice only you can make! Did you two ever have unprotected sex?" I interrogated.

"Did you?" he questioned back.

"Yes, we had unprotected sex a few times." I answered while rolling my eyes.

"We did too." He shamefully answered.

"Lance, what the hell is going to happen? I now have to worry about getting AIDS. This thought along makes me sick to my stomach.

"If it helps, we both tested clean one month ago. When was your last test, Rae?"

"This is too much for me to handle. I do not know about four or five months ago. The results were negative though."

"My head hurts." Ray moaned while rocking side to side and cradling his head in his hand.

Lance and I turned to him and then we turned to each other.

"I don't want him, you can have him." I said.

"Rae, please don't tell my family. Please don't tell Rachel either. She'll be devastated."

"Well Lance, you won't be breaking her heart too bad. You might fuck her head up with this announcement of being gay, but she knew."

"What?"

"She overheard you on the phone that night you found her in your closet on the floor. She heard you talking to Lila!"

"Oh my God" he cried while placing his head into his hands.

"Don't worry, she's a big girl. She was pissed, but she'll get over it. Something like this will take time. You see, Rachel pushed all her frustration out on me, while it should have been you! She was really pissed at you Ray! Just do not rush her to accept any of our bullshit. We both are in the wrong, BIG TIME!"

"You can tell your lover not to ever contact me again. Please Lance, don't pressure me to coming around or calling you. I need time to think about things."

"Rae, I need to talk to you." Ray begged as he struggled to gain his balance while reaching out towards me.

"No, you and Lance can both leave. Lance I need all the keys. You can keep the keys to your summer home in Florida and the keys to all your cars and trucks. You cannot have any keys to my salons. I will have all locks changed by Monday anyways, but for now hand them over."

He gave the keys to me and then he looked directly into my eyes.

"For what it's worth, you are the best woman I ever had Rae"

"No...he is!" I said, as I pointed towards Ray, and then escorted them towards the door.

"Leave now, both of you!" Giving them both vicious stares as they gathered their things and left my salon.

"You okay girl?" Wanda asked as she re-entered the room.

"I will be." Trying not to sound hurt I caught the first tear that had been trying to escape from my eye all evening (*now morning)* long.

"I guess this is the hard part." I said

"What you mean Rae?" Wanda asked while rubbing my back.

"Decontaminating, this filthy sex pit up!" I joked while starring around at my trashed spa room that those three fucks used as a sexual garden of sin!

"Who better to help you out girl?"

"Thanks for being here for me." I said while burying my head into my friends' chest.

No problem, let's get this shit done and go have breakfast; my treat!" she said while tightening up on her hug.

"Damn, I would hope so heifer!"

At this moment, I began to reflect on the prayer I spoke unto the Lord the other night. Its funny how you pray for something, then you finally decide to let go and let God. Did I really want all of this happen? Maybe not in this fashion, but I'm glad the Lord took over, because I don't know what would have happened if I never got on my knees and surrender my problems to the Lord!

Chapter 9:

When One Door Closes…

There have been times where my Will Downing CD could calm me down anytime of the day, but today was not that day. I shake with emptiness and I cry in disbelief. No greatly sung hymn or dramatic sermon, can stir my soul right now. Hell, my mind left me long time ago. The only feeling that lingers around is a feeling called…hopelessness! All I can do is begin to do is thank the Lord that I wasn't dragged even further by my bad foot, to the gates of hell by messing around with Ray. Then I intensify my praises, because it probably would have gotten worse by living with a man who was on the *down low*. God knows what could have happened if I that 'incident' was never discovered.

I leaned over my mile high pile of covers, and started pushing the wine bottles to the side and snatched my clock around back to its rightful position. I was trying to decide what time I planned to re-surface back to the real world. I guess I can't hide in this house forever. One week away from the world was enough. I was so grateful that my sister offered to keep Rachel with her while I try to re-arrange things in the house. I promoted Bella to my salon manager because the girl deserved it. When she rocked Janet's hair the way she did, that confirmed my choice! This is going to be so hard. I just can't imagine where to start. All the anniversaries, the parties, the thought of not having a *family life* were on my mind. Those thoughts soon became a memory, because now…well, I'm on my own.

Just as I place my feet onto the floor my phone rings.

"Desirae!" the crazed voice yelled.

"Yeah, who in the hell is this?"

"Just like a hoe! You don't even remember who you sleep around with!" the irrational voice blazed through the phone.

"Excuse me?" I asked, while recording this voice in my mind and mentally playing it backwards hoping a face matches the voice that soars through my phone!

"It's Anthony Myers!" he angrily shouted.

"What is it Anthony?" I asked sounding more irritated that this punk jock had the nerve to call me after the shit he tried to pull with me, and a teammate of his. I'm too much of a selfish lover to share two men. I want it all- - one on one.

"You got it now bitch!" Anthony sniped.

"What are you talking about? With whom have you been talking with? Do you know something I don't know?" I asked hoping the drama at the salon did not leak out.

"Let me tell you how it starts so you can associate the symptoms with the matter once it makes its appearance! Headaches, sore throat, rashes, fatigue, fever. Do any of these things sound familiar?" he quizzes

"What the fuck are you talking about? I asked, while running to the bathroom to start giving myself my own medical exam.

"I'm HIV positive and I just thought you should know you tramp! I gave my physician the names of ALL my partners, but you are the most suspect of them all."

Suddenly my heart is racing, my speech is slurred; I instantly start to feel weak and dizzy. I can't even pace my thoughts. Scenes of Lance stomping the shit out of me- ***as if he would have the right to do so-***, my family members not ever wanting to talk to me again; my daughter without her mother and finally...scenes from my funeral knock my 20/20 vision right out of my eyeballs! I need to gain some control!

"Hey, I know ***you*** don't actually believe that I am the one that gave this to you. First off, I had a test done four months ago and it was clean. Secondly, you are a PRO- HOE JOCK! All the road trips, the extra scoops of hoes on the side and heaven only know what else; is the reason you caught up! You had better make sure you find your '*dick-ta-phone*' to look up all your flings and start to calling. I'm not to blame for your death sentence!"

"Look bitch, you need to go get tested and prove to me that you are not H.I.V. positive or I will leak this to that husband of yours."

"You have no proof! You can't do that shit." I said.

My mind is racing faster than the horses at the tracks now, because I know Anthony is straight crazy. He performs on impulse, he never thinks out anything he does! Yeah, just like a wide receiver! I got a play he won't see coming.

"Look, I'll have my doctor contact you or I will get a print out from my docs office then we can meet."

"It better be certified results! I want to see actual reports, not a fucking sheet of paper with a check mark in the positive or negative box.' Anthony commanded.

"Whatever! You will take what I give you! I'll make sure you get what you need, and then you can continue on with your search for the skank diva, that passed this shit onto you!"

"Have a nice life you whore, hope you have ***it*** as well. You don't deserve to live for..."

Click~!

I don't even want to hear his bitch ass scream anymore!

My mind was scrambling likes eggs in a skillet, simply because I am trying to remember when our last rendezvous was, but I can't. It is on the borderline of when I had my last HIV test performed. My only question is... was it before or after I had the testing? If it was afterwards, I am in for some hell awful news! I immediately called the doctors office to schedule an emergency appointment.

"Mrs. Lewis you sounded quite upset over the phone"

I was too ashamed to come right out with my news. I paced the floor back and forth until I finally decided to let it out.

"Look thanks for seeing me on such short notice. I 'm very upset because I received a call today that shook me up! One of my old lovers called and informed me that he was HIV positive. I can't remember when the last time we had sex, but I'm terrified and I need to know today!" I stuttered out to the doctor.

"Okay, no problem. Everything will be confidential until..."

"What are you talking about doctor?"

"Well, if your test comes back positive you will have to inform your husband and we will need to see the both of you to set up counselling and to start you on a cocktail of HIV medications. Early treatment is the best defense! *Why is this woman talking to me as if she already knows my results?* We can't leave it up to you alone to report your results to your husband. All outside parties involved must be made aware."

With that information, I suddenly got queasy at the thought of telling my husband...***EX husband*** that I'm HIV positive. Next thing I knew vomit was everywhere.

"Desirae, relax and try to calm down." Dr. Dennison yelled, while grabbing a towel to wipe my face down.

Sweat, then the chills, and finally a spell of shakes took over my entire body. I lay back on the examining table to get rid of my dizzy spells.

"Please do a rapid test now and then I will wait for the final run from your lab. I'm aware that I have to wait for the confirmation test as well. I just need some peace of mind. I want a call the moment the results print off the instrument. I will pay extra for the test to be done stat!"

"Hold out your arm, pump your first, now go ahead and keep your arm straight." She instructed while prepping my arm for the blood draw.

"On the count of three I'll stick. One, two, three, stick."

"Ouch! Damn that hurt! You should've had your phlebotomist do this." I whined.

"Desirae, you voiced great concern, that you wanted this entire visit to be private didn't you? I even keep your medical chart back here with all my celebrity and other V.I.P. clients, locked up in my cabinet! Don't worry, I promise to take care of you girl." She promised, as I watched the blood travel into the vacuumed tube, I prayed that all those blood cells would come back with great news.

"I'll be on my cell phone, please call me when you have results." I said while holding the cotton over the draw site.

As I left the office, I noticed that the sun was bright, the breeze was cool but not freezing, and here I am hotter and sweatier than the entire team of the Miami Heat. Not a damn thing refreshing was in site.

Everyone around me was going on with his or her life, as if all was well. I'm stuck in some fucked up form of translation, or a Matrix moment because shit isn't moving at all. I start thinking, while I'm watching everyone that passes by; that maybe every third or fifth person that walks by me is HIV positive. *Like that is going to help the fucking population.* I can't help but thinking in statistical terms now; because it seems that if my results come back positive, that is all I will be…A FUCKING STATISTIC!

The new *'dilemma'* I've gotten myself into is truly fucking with my mental status right now. I guess so, just knowing you will die sooner than you thought is a crazy thought. Hell, who knows; ***(Okay, now I'm trying to comfort myself***) maybe I was going to die in a week, a month, maybe even a year with or without being HIV positive! Maybe a truck was going to hit me, or maybe by one of my so-called lovers that could not take another one of my ***"I am not leaving my husband"*** responses and shoot me.

This day is one I truly wished would have never came. I'm hurting, tired, depressed and all alone. I am so afraid to look in the mirror at myself right now, because I can't stand to face myself. Is this what I really wanted? I can't even begin to lie and make some off the chain, unrealistic promise to the Lord that if my test came back negative, I would learn my lesson. Just for thinking like that and being a liar, the Lord would probably allow the test to come back positive with a side of syphilis! The most fucked up part about all of this is; I can't help but to think about sex while driving down the street. Do I need help or what?

I know I have a problem and there is only one place to go...THE LORD'S HOUSE!

The Lord has a way of calling his children to the table for a talk. Okay, I got the point! I'm coming back home Lord!

Chapter 10: What Ever Happened to the Other Door Opening?

Shame on people, who feel like the church, should open up its doors, extend its arms, and melt all your troubles away in an instant when you finally decide to show up! I'm double bad, because I simply send my tithes with the hope that, that act alone would shield me like a big umbrella from being missing on Sunday Morning as well as the trials of life. I know I'm wrong but seeing all the folks in the church spinning vicious webs of bullshit so big until it's all out of control and sticky is not for me.

Every woman in the church talking about the first lady, the deacons talking about the ministers and the ministers talking about how they are going to overthrow the Bishop and take over the church is enough to make any lost soul stay away from the church altogether! Oh yeah, lets not forget the folks that damn all the gays and lesbians in the church as well; like we all don't need the love of the Lord. I can't stand altar calls either. The wrong folks go to the altar! Then, when I decide to look up – ***even though every head is bowed and all eyes are closed-*** I can visualize all the snakes slithering out from the side of the pews slithering together to hiss about the ones at the altar!

Every church has drama; there's no sense in trying to shake that fact off like a bad case of dandruff, because it is true! The only reason why I visit with Bishop Thomas and the First Lady because they make themselves available to me at all times. I call from time to time and I vent, cry, seek their counsel, and sometimes look for the rights in my wrongs. I know it is a bad way to think, but can you ever go home without anyone saying something bad? No matter what we discuss in the office, it stays and that means the world to me.

Oh hell, the phone is vibrating its ass off. I'm so scared, but I'd rather know than not know.

"Hello?"

"Miss Lady." The calm and mellow voice whispered.

"Who is this?"

"It's Devin. How's your day going? Was your trip all that you planned on it being?"

"Hello Devin. All went well, but I have come home to some craziness and I have been busy since I got back a little over a week ago. Look, I don't mean to be rude, but I need to call you back."

"Only, if you decide to have dinner with me tonight. I would love to sit down and get to know you a little bit. I told you that at the concert, remember?"

I can't believe I am blushing considering all the shit that I got jogging through my mind.

"Look Devin I have one foot in hells door ad the other probably in a grave. I have too much going on to be..."

"Rae, I haven't met a woman like you since The Lord did his thing and created Eve from Adam. You're right, I don't know you and I am sure there are some things that are so ugly about you that it wouldn't even look good in silk and lace, but I promise to take my time and try to understand. A woman like you with a great man like me is a powerful combination."

Damn, I noticed he said "with a man like me***" not behind,*** a man like me. That shit rung into my ear like a whistle.

"Give me about three weeks to take care of business and to clear my schedule Devin. If you can hold out, I would love to have dinner with you the weekend before the Thanksgiving holiday. Seven pm at the Cheese-cake Factory on the twentieth sound good. The one located at the Galleria Mall. Please be on time, I hate waiting."

Releasing all the air trapped in his body, he finally accepts on my terms.

"You got it sweetness. I'll be on time, and the reservation will be made under the Anderson Party."

"Okay." I agreed.

"Rae?"

"Yes Devin." I answered trying not to sound like I was pre-occupied.

"You never asked me why I seem to be so interested in you."

"You did tell me Devin." I giggled.

"When did I say that?"

"The concert, remember? You said you could smell me in the air!"

Damn my panties got wet with that thought!

"Please don't focus on that night. I generally don't get down with my women like that. I told you your vibe, your essence and a certain amount of pride you contained made my dick grow beyond measure. You also sent many cosmic neurons firing from my brain throughout my entire body!" *Does he really think that I'm going to believe he will not roll his dick out like a red carpet every time he sees a fine woman?*

"Really, you don't say?" I asked while trying to focus on my driving.

"I want you to listen to this poem a brother by the name of Ausar wrote."

"Ausar? I have heard of that name before."

"Yeah he's a poet here in the Lou."

"Okay, I caught him performing at Mocha Latte's "Got Lyrics?" joints. I love his poetry!"

"Well just listen to this because it will explain how I feel about you. For a long time I've been listening to my friends talk about you."

"Me? Explain how Devin." I interrupted, trying to figure out how his friends and I know of each other.

"Well, my friends have wives and girlfriends that frequent your shop and from that point, the conversations started. I've heard of all the work you perform in the community and how well people receive you."

"Go on. You got me nervous now. A sister got a couple hundred haters just on one block, so what's up?"

"Baby, the word is all good! People really respect and love you. You have a sweet spirit. It's nice to hear a group of people that can say the same thing about an individual. It means that people really respect and admire you."

"I'm flattered." I had to look in my rear view mirror because I know I had a silly assed grin on my face.

"Well there you go. I fell in love with you by ear! I fell in love with everything I heard about you."

"Stop, your making me blush my ass off."

"When I saw you at the concert, I instantly said the media should be fired for how they represented you, because the pictures they took of you do you no justice!"

"You're too much." *Damn, there goes a good pair of panties!*

Why do I feel like pulling over right now and start *loving* on myself? This man sure knows how to erect all of my senses.

"Listen up, you ready for this poem?" Devin proudly announces.

"Spit that shit out my brother."

"You "

"Look at You,
behold You,
the shape of You.
A gorgeous woman...
that You.

Beautiful You,
sexy You,
delightful You.
The one that captures my eye...
is You.

The feel of You,
the grip of You,
the squeeze of You,
is what I get in the arms of You.

When I kiss, there's You.
When I hug, there's You.
When I touch, there's You.
Making love to only You.

When I asleep, there's You.
When I awake, there's You.
When I think, there's You.
In my dreams, there's You.

The shoulder I cry on is You.
The ear I bend on is You.
The balance I weigh on is You.
On whose love I depend on is You.

The cause of my smile is You.
The cause of my laughter is You.
The cause of joy is You.
The one that I love is You.

The reason I live
is You.
All that I have

I wish to give to You.

In the morning
there's You.
In the afternoon
there's You.
In the evening
there's You.
Thru all the arguments,
trials & tribulations.
Thru all the disappointments
still there is no leaving you.

I'll die for You,
kill for You.
And when I lay with You,
I'll thrill for You!

I'll tickle You
and tease You.
Lick You
and squeeze You.
Flip, toss & turn You.
I'll do it all...
just to please You!

I'll grind with You,
69 with You.
Seek & find new ways

to blow your mind

with You!

I'll lay my heart on the line for You.

Promise to be mindful to...

Love, Honor, and Treasure You.

Hug, Kiss, and Pleasure You.

Maintain, Protect, and Defend You.

From now...

until my life ends with You."

By: Ausar

"You like?" Devin asked.

"You really feeling on me like that?"

"Yes." Devin moaned.

"I'm touched." I said while gently massaging my nipples.

"See you in three weeks Devin!"

"Good bye." Devin whispered before hanging up.

That is some deep shit there. Falling in love before you actually meet that person is some deep shit. How can I even begin to want to fall into something when I barely made it out of the trap that caught me up for years?

I was starting to feel good until the damn phone started vibrating again. I'm aware that the caller could be about only one thing...LIFE OR DEATH!

"Hello."

"Rae, its Dr. Dennison."

"I tried catching you before you whirl winded yourself out the office, to inform you of your rapid test..."

"Well why didn't you fucking call me? I'm sure you can understand how fucked up my mind and my nerves are right now!" I said while frantically searching for one of those stale ass cigarettes from my old smoking days.

"Rae, your rapid came back negative, so since that looked pretty good I delivered your specimen to the lab; and personally handed the specimen over to my sister Jennifer. She's a medical tech in the lab. I just got her call a few minutes ago, and sweetie...your negative!"
The tears started to flow from my eyes uncontrollably.

"Thank the Lord" I rejoiced while hitting the steering wheel while I crushed up the cigarette.

Thank heaven my windows on my car were tinted. I looked trashed like bad meat out the refrigerator. My nose was runny with strings of snot, my eyes were bloodshot, I was so pale, and my hair? Just fuck it; take away my cosmetologist license today! No make-up or fresh do can hide the drama that I have been through recently. No matter how I try to hold on, sometimes letting go of it, all is best, even though it hurts like hell!

"Rae? Are you there?"

"I'm here. Thank you! I appreciate all of your help."

"It's not over Rae, you need to get counselling and you need some time for you! Take time for Rae. You have been through a lot lately and you need to take the time to get your mind right. Please don't make the mistake and think that you can get this all on your own. I'm calling in a script to the pharmacy and I want you to start these meds, ASAP!"

"Will they take the *Rae* out of me?"

"No, but they will give you mental balance and mellow you out. Please go see this doctor as well. I really care about you, but now is the time for you to take a different direction with your life style choices."

"Okay, I will do it."

"Great, I want to see you in two weeks. You will be monitored like this until I feel you're on the right path!"

"Thank you so much for all of your help, time and efforts on my behalf. I'm looking forward to doing some things different in my life. I just need to figure out the plan and go from there. Will you please email me the information because I'm driving right now?"

I have a second chance. The Lord truly does love this child of his. I guess now would be a good time to make sure the first lady is at the church and available to see me. I know she will not be too happy to hear from me under these circumstances, considering the fact I haven't been to church since Easter!

"Thanks for calling West End Baptist Church, what has the Lord done for you today?"

"Jamie?" I asked.

"Rae? Girl where you been? You know I am gone transfer you right on in to the first lady so she can deal with you. I miss seeing you, and your family. When yall coming by?"

"We will drop by in due time. I need to speak with the first lady and I'm only ten minutes from the church. Is she busy?"

I hate when folks try to get all in your damn business. Hell, if it were not for her ass working at the church she wouldn't be there either.

"Just stop on by. She just finished the literacy program with the youth. She'll be very happy to see you."

"Great, tell her I'm on my way."

I decided to call that punk assed Anthony Meyers on the way to the church to inform him of my test results, so he can hear for himself that my results are negative. In addition, I had my doctor to call him as well. I don't trust him with any thing. I know he would leak a rumor to everyone he knows here in the Lou, just to ruin (as if it cannot get any worse) my life. I also threw a touchdown by threatening him right back to expose his shit, if he even mentions us having an affair. I promised to release Maurice on him. He hates Maurice with a passion. I told him I planned to let Maurice on spread a vicious rumor that he is Anthony's gay lover and he wants to help him come out of the closet! The NFL will shit all on his ass! There is nothing worse than a bitch ass dude!

As I sat across from the first lady telling her my story, I could feel a break down on the way. Her looks of disappointment were so strong to the point where they overpowered my soul. I felt like a demon in flight.

"Why are you looking at me like that First Lady?"

"You have some releasing to do. The only way anyone can move from what they are currently dealing with is to announce the problem, then make sure you mean what you have said!

I know she don't want me to get ugly in the Lords' house!

"I'm Desirae Lewis… and I'm addicted to sex." I boldly stated.

"There…is that the release you wanted?" I yelled forgetting all of my church mannerisms.

"No, Desirae I don't want to hear that!"

"Then what, *do* you want to hear? I yelled, as I threw my hands into the air, with a look of panic and desperateness.

"I can't do this shit!"

"Rae, you will respect me ***and* the HOUSE OF THE LORD!"** First Lady yelled, while wiping her face for the millionth time, with her lace handkerchief.

Too ashamed to look directly into the first lady's eyes, I looked downward as I continue to humble myself and speak on.

"I hurt many people behind my secrete lifestyle, but you want to know what really hurts? I asked while rocking back and forth with my feet barley planted on the floor.

"Tell me child."

"What hurts the most is…I lost the ones I loved." I said as I hugged myself, while allowing a few tears of regret to flow.

"Where will you go from here? Do you think you can be happy with the choices you have made? The first lady questions, as she taps her swollen foot on the floor.

"Well…I asked you a question!"

Feeling a sudden rush of heat, more tears flow from my eyes, confusion and frustration burst loose.

"I…I, don't want to discuss this in the church. I feel uncomfortable. They need to get the crime scene tape out, because what I've done is a KILLER act!"

"Well if you feel like that then we need to continue your healing right, here! This way, you won't be so tempted to stray from the truth. Rae, it's bad to lie, but even worse to do it in Gods house." She reaches for my hand, but I pull away.

"I feel uncomfortable talking about my life, sex, and anything in regards to me, at the moment!" For some reason it seemed that the only thing that could catch me today was the floor.

I fell onto the marbled floor as if was going to absorb all my shame and guilty acts. The tears continued to flow uncontrollably until I found myself in a puddle of shame.

"I'm an adulterer, a whore, a liar, a flat out sinner!" I yelled, while shivering beyond my control.

"Baby, you need to calm down! Don't give into what the devil wants," she said while hovering over me, laying a blanket of love and warmth over me, that I've not felt in a long time.

"You give yourself to the Lord all will be well. Let go, and let God work child! Once you learn to release the thoughts that you are in control, God will step in and show out! We think we run things, but baby you know we don't." First Lady shouted while throwing much praise to the heavens. Standing up to gather my things, while wiping the tears away and shaking off the last of my shivering spell, I instantly paused and turned to the first lady.

"If you are a so-called *First Lady* following the word of the Lord, then I advise YOU to do whatever necessary to sure my soul is not lost!"

At that instant, what I thought would take years and a great weight loss plan; the First Lady instantly pounces into my face, as if she was going to strike me.

"No baby, YOU are responsible for YOUR own soul!" she cried, while looking at me in pure disgust.

She struggles to maintain her three hundred pound frame onto her tired, swollen feet.

"The church is where we learn doctrine, worship and praise the Lord. It also provides shelter, jobs, and other services for the community. It's different if you were innocent and you were out here being responsible, but look at how you've been acting child! You are held for your actions and there is always a price to pay for your sins!"

Now so close in my face, I can tell she keeps a handbag full of those red and white star mints. I guess it is better than funk!

"The church can't do it all Rae-Rae. We give you the tools, the resources to learn of the world so that you do not get caught-up in worldly episodes, like an endless soap opera. When the show is over, judgment will occur. You'll be the only one on stage. Will your light shine, or will your light be substituted for a flame of fire?"

She puts her good eye on me while studying me; because she knows I am about to put her faith and strength, through a true test!

"Fine, but don't expect me to fly out of here with wings and a halo on my head just from one session!" I smarted off, while pretending to fly around her office like a fallen angel.

"You think I've always been a First Lady?" she questioned.

"Honestly?"

"Can you tell it to me like the good word, Rae?"

"Yes, even better."

"Don't flatter yourself child. Nothing is sweeter than the word of MY LORD!" she proclaims as she throws her hands upwards towards the heavens.

"Quit rushing me. You church folk always in a hurry for the truth to be told, knowing yall can't handle it!"

"Back at you child!" she hissed while cutting her eyes at me.

"No, I don't think that's the case. I know most people God appoint to his ministry have been through some very hellish experiences. All the suffering, the drugs, the hooking and God know what else, before he finally extends his hands for that an invitation to have a chance at being saved."

"Oh, so you know the deal?"

"Yes, but am I really at my end? Have I suffered enough? Is God done with me?"

I begin to pound into my chest as if a drum sat upon it, hoping some sweet beats of relief would tunnel through my spirit and soar out of my mouth.

"Rae, are you ready to face your future? God has allowed you to escape, the wrath and fury of AIDS. What price were you really prepared to pay, for sleeping around on your husband?"

The guilt is crushing me. Every time I try to stand, I feel the force of guilt pushing me downward. Why is it, that no matter how hard you try to paint the scene or tell the story, people never understand what you are going through until they step into your shoes? I can't understand the pressure of what it's like, not to have a pot to piss in, a lousy paying job, past due bills *and* a child with a disability. I can never tell someone who is going through some shit like that, "It's gone be all right." I've never had to walk that road, so I would be wrong to tell someone that I understand what he or she is going through. I don't expect anyone to do a damn thing for me. I know I have to make this trip alone, because I'm one of a kind, with a whole bowl of problems.

"Please help me LORD!" I cried, while rocking back and forth, shielding my shameful face from the first lady. There I was, crying like a newborn baby, wanting its mother.

"Once again the warmth and sweet smell of forgiveness showered my soul. The rock is rolling over, but there is still slight pressure. Maybe it was the fear of moving on which was weighing heavily upon my back

"Rae, do you forgive yourself?"

"Yes."

"Are you positive? You're not just saying this because you have been busted and practically lost all that once loved you before, are you?"

"No ma'am." I replied as I wiped my face clean.

"I know God has unconditional love for me, and I can't worry about what others think. I can only try to improve and re-start my life. I still have my baby girl."

"Well how are things between you and Rachel?"

"We've talked and she seemed to understand everything. I have been home more, and I have made so many plans for us.

"What about Mr. Lance."

"Lance? That's over. No dipping back into that pot even if it was full of greens with smoked hammocks!"

"Oh, Rae, don't make me put no greens on in the middle of the week." The first lady teased while rubbing her already full belly.

"I know where he stands and I can't continue to put myself in harms way. It was enough that I was out here being reckless, but to add to what he was doing, well...that leaves no room for discussion."

"All I can do is on hold. In the meantime, I will have to do some soul searching. I hate to even think about possibilities at a time like this, but there is a man that has caught my attention."

"Child, you're some kind of crazy!" she yelled while swatting me with the yellow velour like pillow from the couch.

"Hey that hurt!" I said while trying to make sure my hair stood in place. I know I look like a hot damn mess, didn't need anything else to tear my look up even more.

"I hope it knocked some sense in that jug head of yours! Whoever he is..."

"I don't plan on a relationship right now. Calm down. I just need someone to converse with, in my time of need. He seems to want to listen as well as take the time to get to know me!"

"You need to talk to Jesus!" First Lady shouted.

"I got him on speed dial too!" I joked, but I could tell she didn't like that joke, because she swung dead for my head.

"Ya missed me!" I teased.

"Well his caller Id gone be broke when you call ***AND*** your prayers ***ain't*** getting answered."

"Come on a give me a hug Shirley. I love you so much." I said while running dead into her arms. Feels just like the hugs momma used to give to me.

"Baby I love you too. The Lord will see you through, but please make sure you get your self some help. I want us to gather at least two times a week for prayer. I need you to be here Rae."

"I will." I promised. *Wait---did I just make a promise?*

"Regular Sunday attendance won't hurt you either! With all you have been through, you should be here before the church doors open on Sunday morning."

"Okay. I'll be there with bible in one hand and my tambourine in the other."

"Hey, don't lie to me. I need you here so that I can lay hands on you."

"No problem, my soul desires it deeply." I truthfully confessed.

'God Blesses ***in his time*** Rae."

Pulling away from the church, I felt a new sense of direction. Nothing in this life is promised but the end, so what direction will I live life in until then? Time will tell. It's too early for me to say. I know there will be times when I'll want to go left when I know I want to go right!

The fall breeze is not as fierce as it was earlier when I left the doctors office. The breeze had a hint of forgiveness attached to it. Is this how refreshing starting over feels?

My Souls Desires are worth hell! I can't turn back!

~Chapter 11~

The Worst Enemy

Damn, a time sure does fly by when you are having fun. Rachel and I had had a little mother daughter time and we bout cleared the stores out! I attended some of her games, dance recitals, and even slowed down my activities at the salon. That child of mine is going to be a straight diva, just like her momma! She's even more than what I prayed for, while carrying her in my womb.

Therapy at the new doctor was very helpful, but oh so damn extensive. That woman probably worked in a coalmine once before or something, because she was digging all into my sexual history. Chapter after chapter of my life; she opened me up as wide as some of my past lovers once did. I had to learn what triggered my sexual impulses. Was it my high sex drive with a side of low self-esteem, or was I truly a sex addict? My therapist explained to me, that I was indeed a person that displayed signs of someone with a hyperactive sex drive.

I also learned that the term nymphomaniac played out years ago in the medical field. It is associated in the streets; because that is the term, we use to associate with the act of a super horny person. Okay, whore too. My doctor was very kind and understanding. She answered all of my questions. Now that some light shines on this topic, I don't feel like a total street whore. I came to understand that my genital area was in need for constant stimulation like a crack baby needing to be held and soothed at all times.

Now that I reflect back to all my sexual escapades, the sex was okay but my appetite continuously re-surfaced. Being very or even partially stimulated, whether it was mentally or physically only increased my need of sexual stimulation. All of this only heightened my physical and mental symptoms. Sooner rather than later, a fucking from someone was soon to follow. Now the sad part about all of this was when she told me my disorder was knocking on the doors of having a bipolar disorder. Meaning I simply regretted each sexual experience, (I really did) which would send me into a deep depressive state. I can now see where the mood swings came from that Lance scolded me about a million times repeatedly.

I had some blood drawn. They wanted to check my dopamine level. If my dopamine levels were unbalanced, then the mystery was over. It was determined that hyperactive sexuality is a side effect of dopamine imbalance. Lord, let that BE THE REASON. I can't be bipolar; crazy is just my stage act when I am trying to get my point across, not the real Rae!

When I think of all my sexual desires, they were so strong that the longest and hardest dick couldn't keep a bitch like me down. I knew it was bad once I started missing family outings, leaving work to go have sex, or being '*turned on'* with one simple look at my Marcella iron.

Okay, that's sick. I know someone would call in a script to the drug store stat, if I told him or her this shit. See the fucked up ones, NEVER think shit is wrong with them. It's everyone else who is wrong for not wanting to fuck 24/7! To me, it wasn't a curling iron; it was a long piece of hot steel, which equalled a long hard dick. Hell, you would have thought my hand was a fern the way I kept it planted in my pussy! See, just when I thought it was cool to pleasure self constantly, I realized there's a limit to shit! I was way over my limit!

There were times when I was in so much pain to where sex seemed impossible but once the thought traveled around my mind in Tsunami like waveform. My sexual urges overpowered my brain and instantly washed out all my restraint. I guess my mind was telling me that I was enjoying the sex or that I really liked whom I was fucking at the time.

Hell this shit is too confusing for my little brain to decipher. I'll leave that job for the real doctors. This shit I'm dealing with is the reason why people should seek professional mental help. Who can talk me through getting over dick? This can't be shit but an *'exhale party'*, and nothing else. Then after everyone leaves, I'm all on my own. Shaking, rocking and crying, while swinging the dick away! Friends and family are not professional help. There's too much out there. One oversight of a sudden symptom or sign and it could be someone's life, ending very soon! I hope my next sexual encounter will really be true in all aspects of desire, physical attraction and mental stability; which will make me chose my lover instead of lusting after my lover.

I realized that I was due to meet Devin in four hours at the Cheesecake Factory for dinner; and I am in dire need of a sprucing! I actually had a very special glow about myself. I felt so damn good and to my surprise, it didn't have shit to do with a side of dick either. Part of my feelings rested upon the new medication that the doctor prescribed, but the other half had to be about my newfound love of...self. While Rachel and I were out shopping last week, I came across a book that blew my mind. The title,

"Breathe Again" caught my attention, and from there, I couldn't stop reading.

I was shocked at the fact that the author- O'Shea- is a St. Louis native. I'll have to check her book tour schedule out. I would love to meet her.

That sister went through a lot of shit and the sad part about it all is that she didn't have access to half the luxuries I have in my own life. It's hard to go through life dealing with all your mental and social issues, while having no financial stability to make life seem a little easier. I would've thrown myself over the mountaintop on the first episode. Yeah, money wouldn't have made all the difference, but it helps! Trust me though, rich don't mean shit when the simple elements in your life look fucked up too. Rich folk got problems too- **TRUST ME!**

Lack of love for self is the worst enemy a person can have! Momma said it best when she said, "It will make you do whatever at any cost, to please everyone else!" My days of that are over.

My goal is to continue to take my meds as prescribed and live life one day at a time. Damn I sound like an ex- junkie or some shit! This just proves a point that everyone suffers with some form of addiction!

I looked up and saw my sister pulling her Navigator into my driveway.

"Rachel, you auntie is outside blowing. Gather your things and make sure you guys call when you reach grandmas house. I'll fly in on Sunday evening and we ***WILL NOT*** be staying the whole seven days! So don't even ask!"

"Okay. Just make sure you and dad can get along at the dinner. Are you and dad going to tell grandma and paw -paw that dad loves to play in fairy dust?" she quizzed while pretending to blow some imaginary dust.

"Watch your damn mouth!"

"Sorry."

"No, we're keeping thangs quiet. No one wants to hear, that your dad and I have separated during the holidays. I don't want that to be the focus."

"That will be for us to do at a later time." I announced.

"If they ask where I am at, remember..."

"Yes, I know. Running your Chicago salon and tending to other business! It's almost tax season and you gotta get ready!"

"Okay, don't be so smart, where you goof up and tell the wrong story."

"I shouldn't be lying anyways, right?" Rachel smarted off.

"Rachel, get to stepping before my hand suddenly becomes attached to your behind." I yelled while crazily rolling my eyes to the good Lord.

"Okay, love you mom." She yells as she flies past me.

"Love you too."

I wasn't really feeling Thanksgiving dinner with Lance and his family, considering the last time I saw Lance was about a month ago. I know there will be no feelings of desire in my tank for his ass. His last act exhausted all the fumes I was riding on from the plane trip to back home. I just don't know what will come to mind once I see him. I know everyone has dealt with this dilemma at a certain time or two in their lives.

I want to let go and let God do what he knows best, but something tells me I won't be so forgiving and in the mood to let go once I see Lance.

~Chapter 12~

Flowing Like Water

Everything flows better in life if you just learn to relax. The time flew by and date night with Devin was here. I stopped by the salon and had Maurice hook me up from head to toe. I was in dire need of his services, and I knew that his "Melt the World Away" mud bath was just what I needed. Yeah, my system was in severe need of a good assed detoxifying session. I'm so glad I didn't let the whole thought of getting a makeover persuade me to cut off my damn hair! This will not be a '***Waiting to Exhale'*** moment! Angela Bassett should have kept her hair. Shit, if I think on this too long India Arie will step in and tell me "***I am not my hair***!" While I relaxed in the tub, my mind couldn't help but to wonder how Ray was doing. Hell, he's probably decided that my ex-husband is the one he wants to spend an eternity loving. I feel like such a damn fool.

"Stop thinking bout them!" Maurice yells, while he's stomping his foot on the ground; and swaying his hands in the air, trying to shoo my mind away from all the drama at hand.

"What are you talking of Reese?"

"Look, Mazy Rae, (his nick name for me) I know you hurt and all girl, but you know that ain't any type of shit you want to be walking back into. You can't make either one of those ass holes yours baby, trust me!"

"I know, but I feel hurt, stupid and so betrayed." I said while swaying my legs from side to side in the thick mud. This is the first time Reese and I had a good sincere talk in a while. I love his confidence and the way he just accepts the way shit is with people. His love them or leave them mentality seems to work for him.

"You know, I think I'll be better once I accept what all has happened."

"Girl I think you have, I just think you scared to step on out there." He said while popping ever so viciously on some gum.

"You know God really has your back. I mean be real, take the time to think bout all the shit you've been through these last few months and tell me if being here right now with me ain't a blessing." He said as he got up to go grab some more towels.

"You are so right."

"I just want to make sure that whatever happens in the future is what *I* want, and also what God wants. We all have a tendency on doing things WE think are good for us, while excluding God. Hell, the only time we seek him is when we need him to fix our mess."

"Please no preaching on Saturdays in the salon girlfriend." Maurice yells as he starts his holy stomp and shouting fest.

"You're a hot damn mess Reese!"

"Don't forget the side order of damn fool too!" he joked.

"Well what about this Devin dude? Do you think I should blow him off?"

"NO! I saw his ass recently and oh my damn gurl! That is a one hundred percent full-blooded man! Those pics he sent to you on your phone...BULLSHIT! He's much better looking in person!" he professed while cheesing from ear to ear.

"Reese, where did you see him at? I asked while sitting straight up.

"He was at Levin's Hat Shop yesterday. He must have been looking for a nice hat for yall date or something. I ran in there, because I needed a hat real bad cause (he lifts the hat up off his head and a porcupine looking creature made of hair, jumps out) of this shit! Girl, I hate taking braids down! It takes forever!"

"Okay, put that back on, DAMN!"

"Any damn who." Maurice snaps while rolling his eyes. I walked by and gave him my '*You on*?" look."

"Well?" I urged.

"That man gave me the most polite but at the same time "Bitch, I'm not on your *"Queen Team"* stare back! Then I tried to push up on him back in the fitting area, and girl he grabbed his hat went to the cashier and that was all I saw of Mr. Man."

"You didn't see any honey drippings or sugar around his lips?" Maurice bout fell into the tub while trying to add more warm water to the mud mix.

"Not one drip at all! Honey I had the pleasure of running into that fine man several times before you even told me about him and he is no joke! He seems to be in and out a lot of the business offices downtown on Washington Ave. I'm positive he is involved with some type of investment firm. Once you showed me his pics and told me about yalls fling; I had my Uncle Darrell conduct a background check on him."

"Are you serious Maurice?" I queried.

"Yeah, you know I be suspect about these fun boys I fuck with now a days, so thank heaven Uncle Darrell still got his P.I. biz. Consider this payback for me messing up that Fendi bag of yours!"

"You want the scoop?" Maurice asked.

"Bitch, don't play with me." I snapped while giving him my infamous look of death!

"He's a cut above the rest. No kids, no ex- anything, no run- INS with the cops and he's super rich!" Maurice said while bending over touching his toes while he shook his ass!

"Baby, show me this is how you gone be for that fine assed mystery book looking brother, when he finally tries to bed you down in private!" Maurice continued to joke while touching his toes.

"Well, looks like he was totally honest. Oh well. I'll just take it slow, I can't be jumping into another relationship so fast, but I can grab a sample here and a sample there."

"That's my girl." Maurice said while standing back to his six-foot one frame.

"Don't go throwing good meat out. You know your momma would whip your ass for running away a good man.," he said while cleaning his skin with one of my facial scrub pads.

As I lay in the warm mud, I can feel my entire body start to melt and dissolve into the mud. I looked upward and the ceiling instantly became a movie screen. Scenes of my mother sitting in the bathroom on the toilet while I'm in the tub, chit chatting the day away, made my eyes well up with tears. I miss those times. Momma could talk me through a cement wall! It didn't matter what I was going through, momma made it all seem like nothing. I could *feel* my mother and even smell her soft, sweet scent of vanilla and jasmine. The tears just started to flow. Everything she told me has come to past.

There we were, Reese sitting on the edge of the tub rubbing my back while yelling," Let it out girl!" as I sat in the warm mixture of mud crying until all my tear wells ran dry.

"I don't believe I've cried like that in a long ass time." I whined uncontrollably, while strings of snot ran from my nose.

"Rae, don't let one, hell, *no man* stop you from living and believing in true love. You were on the right path when you were planning to spilt with your husband. The Lord just had to make it be a way, where you could never go back. Sometimes, we're too stupid to remove ourselves from certain situations, so the Lord just steps in and does it for us. Here girl, get ya face right. This is *so* not sexy!"

"Thanks so much Reese." We hugged until I thought I was passing out, or turning into a puff of smoke. Talk about being tight! I need some air.

"Oh, shit!" I jumped while looking at the clock on the wall.

"What's wrong Rae?"

"I only got one hour to get dressed to go to the Galleria."

"Girl gets to moving. I will clean up and lock the place up for you. You can't be late."

"Thanks! I really do love you Reese."

Looking at me with a slight look of disappointment Maurice finally gives in to one of his room brightening smiles and confesses.

"That would sound so much better coming from Shamar Moore, or Boris Kudjoe, but I feel ya sista girl."

I guess I better get prepared to pay this high ass water bill, because I am allowing my life to flow on non-stop.

~Chapter 13~

Men All Pause

"I need twenty on pump seven and ring this water and gum up also please."

"Is there anything else for you Miss Lady?" the tired faced, and desperate looking clerk asked.

"No, I'm fine."

"That you are. You look like you are about to have a very special evening. I'm so jealous of that lucky guy!" he said while viewing all my angles and curves as if he was preparing for an algebra quiz.

I blushed and I was feeling a lil embarrassed. Everyone in the gas station had his or her eyes on me.

"Thanks so much, but trust me when I say there is no need for jealousy. Eventually some woman will be jazzing herself up for you, while some other man will be telling her the same thing you rapping to me. Have a great evening."

I couldn't help but notice that all eyes were on me. One man was pumping way more than his gas tank could hold and all the gas was just gushing out onto him. If I stood there with a match flaming on the stick, that idiot wouldn't stop pumping.

Then there was always a group of haters, but I got a cure for that dreaded disease and the people who have it.

It is called- - - NICENESS!

"Hello my sisters, how you all doing tonight?"

"Heeeeeey." they all respond in a faint and fake assed tone of voice. They all turn back around to talk amongst each other. I guess they were trying to figure out who was paying for the gas, so they can cruise the night away looking for *new* baby daddies.

I've learned not to give into negative energy. Just kill them with kindness. My relationship with most people outside of my life is like a new meal on the menu at McDonalds…for a limited time only bitches!

I'm feeling so damn good I have to put my 'Sexy Back' CD on. Oh, please do not trip and think I am referring to that young white boy with the last name of Timberlake. I'm talking bout those sexy divas from way back then…KLYMAXX!

Speeding on highway I-70 with my rims reflecting silver streaks of lighting off the highway lights as I zoomed by the airport, gave an alert to other cars that I was on a mission. The music was so loud and thunderous that my back felt the massage from the pulsating beats that vibrated onto my back, into my spinal column, and then they finally filtered right into my soul. From there, I could not hold back any longer. I finally had to join in and sing with the first Divas of Sexy.

"Cause I know I'm Looking good I'm givin' attitude all over the room

People starin' at me I just look too good for these people *(I can't help but to lean back in my seat and bust out with the snake, DAMN talk about an old school dance move.)*

"***I am feeling too good and looking too damn sexy!"***

"Don't you know the men all pause yeah; just look at them (Woof) the dog is coming out of them natural dog radar (woof) Whoa, Whoa, Whoa, /////// WHOA!" I screamed out the lyrics like an American Idol contestant at its worst; while checking my rear and side view mirrors, trying to preserve my sexy, like Diddy.

Damn I just did my five min workout in the front seat of my ride. I didn't know I could pop and lock like that! Okay, let me stop before I have to take another bath again. Ah, who is this interrupting my concert?

"Hello?"

"Rae, please listen and don't hang up."

"Raymond, why are you calling me?" I asked while turning down my radio and parking my car on the lot of the galleria.

"I've been trying to call you, I've come by your salon a few times, and even tried to find your sister; hoping she would set me up with you for a meeting."

"See, Jesus really loves you Ray!" pointing my finger out the window as if I were really talking to him.

"What are you talking about Rae?"

"If you would have approached my sister, you would be missing right now. Don't you think she is aware about you and the entire file, back sliding shit you have not only done to me... but my entire family?"

"Rae, look allow me to tell you the truth."

"What do you plan on telling me that will make me change what I think and how I feel about you Raymond?" I asked while punching in on my dashboard. There goes the thought of not giving into negative shit as well as a beautiful manicure.

"Look I am in my church study and I promise you, I wouldn't be sitting in the Lords house of worship telling you a lie."

"Bullshit! I know plenty of people that sit in church every Sunday looking for the rights in their wrongs, praying and promising God what they will and will not do. Things like promising to tithe, not back sliding anymore; to stop drinking, whoring, and smoking crack, dreaming of sleeping with the pastor or first lady and heaven only knows what else. The Lord must have an entire army of secretaries to keep up with all the lies that people make- - - IN CHURCH ON SUNDAY MORNING!

"Rae, I can't worry about anyone else. What I know is being a minister, a child of the Lord and most of all… a man, I must make amends, or try anyways for what I've done. I am trying to give you as well as myself a final end to this sad part of our lives."

Looking at my watch, my mind drifts to a lovely dinner with Devin and a nice helping of Key Lime cheesecake!

"Look, I have a meeting right now and time is not on your side right now. I'll call you when I am on my way out of town. I'm only allowing you thirty minutes to make your peace, or shall I say…make yourself feel better."

"Thanks- - -"I had to hang up on his ass. I'm so *NOT* into him.

Who said you had to be nice all the time!

~Chapter 14~

Dinner for Two

Hi, I'm here for the Anderson party please."

"Right this way please." The waiter responds, while giving me a nod that my crème colored, cashmere cat suit, with my gold sequined crop jacket highlighted by my gold
Jimmy Choo's, was a better choice than any specialty they had on their menu tonight.

Walking over I instantly spotted Devin and to hell with the cheesecake. He could be my dessert. He stands out and outfits this entire restaurant like the art; they have displayed on the walls. I suddenly feel flushed with a moderate amount of heat and I can't help but to blush my ass off. I noticed all the men and even some women staring at me. One sister elbowed her date in the side and demanded to know "What the hell you looking at!" as I strutted through the restaurant. All I can think about is the night at the concert.

The way Devin dropped to his knees and started to feed off me was a thought that could possibly send me into a re-lapse phase of me fighting off dick like a bad case of the cold or flu. Never had a brother talk to the pussy the way he did!

"Hello there Mr. Anderson, I take it you have already ordered our food and drinks." I said while giving him my look of approval.

I couldn't help but to wonder if my outfit was too extreme or if my hair being combed over to one side showing my beautifully sculpted swan like neck accented by my gold and diamond braided necklace was too much. The way he stared then looked around was nerve wrecking. Seconds later, he instantly put my fear to sleep.

"You look like royalty. All of this for me?" he said as he took to his feet like a real man.

"No, for me my dear man, but you are certainly welcome to some." I said as I leaned inward to kiss him on his clean-shaven, and bump free face.

"I am so happy you chose to have dinner with me tonight, please…sit with me." He motioned for me to sit in the seat across from him. We both must have had the intent on staring each other down, so sitting across from him was just perfect.

After a few cups of coffee and many jokes, the mood settled and there we were eye to eye and my mind went blank. I can't recall myself feeling like this with Lance when we were dating. I feel free, unrestricted and at ease with this man. Damn, please let something fall from the sky into my lap to tell me this shit will not work.

"You know Rae; I want you to understand one thing."

"What's that Devin?"

"I generally don't indulge in any woman the way I did with you on the night of the concert. There was something that grabbed a hold of my mind and I knew that was a battle that I was not going to win."

"You and that dick of yours should have a talk." I joked.

"Trust me; we've already had that talk and I see you still got more jokes for me."

"Okay, I will stop with the jokes." I said laughing uncontrollably.

"I have waited all of my life for a woman that I could connect with in more than just a sexual way. I felt more than a sexual connection between us when we met. I could see your soul dancing with excitement through your eyes."

"Devin, please wait..."

"No, I do believe you have to wait your turn."

"Okay, go on."

"I'm aware that you have some issues about yourself, that may not be as appealing as the very image that sits before me tonight, but what I want is for us to take things slow, get to know one another and let love flow like water over the falls!"

"Okay, here is what you need to know and this is in no random order. Lance and I have separated; we are in the process of a divorce. An ex-lover threatened me with news that I could be H.I.V. positive and the man whom I was cheating on my husband with was fucking my husband. Oh, please let me also inform you that the night I caught them in my New York salon having sex; I caught my best friend there as well.

Unmoved by all the shit I said he had one question.

"How do you feel now?"

"I feel so relieved."

"How being?" he asked while taking another sip of coffee.

"Well, I know that I am not H.I.V. positive, my husband turning out being gay was probably the best thing that has ever happened to me, my daughter and I have strengthened our relationship and I feel so in love with myself once again. I really feel confident about my future."

"Damn, that's what I love bout you Miss Lady." Devin responded while flashing his beautiful smile.

"What is that, if I may ask?"

"Your vibe, the magical flow you have and the confidence of a fierce lioness. You have a true love Jones for your own self. That thought alone there is beautiful. A woman, who loves herself, will not allow the negativity of other people or the world break her stride is a portrait of beauty."

I can't even finish the meal placed before me, because this man has fed my soul. I sure as hell hope there's not a wet spot on this seat when I get up!

"You know what my soul desires?" I asked, as I took one last sip of my coffee.

"What? Tell me what a beautiful soul like yours desire?" he said while alerting the waiter for the check.

"It desires for a man to recognize my strength, my essence, my womanhood, my fearlessness, and the way I hold things down; without being intimidated. My soul desires the need for a *real* man to step up to the plate, accept me as I am and not try to halt my dreams like the traffic police. I need my man to stand beside me when I need him; then on certain occasions I may need him to fall back to give me my space ***but*** never leave me! I need him to understand that I am a woman that requires regular feedings, sexually, spiritually and mentally. Please tell me that you can do all of this."

Without much thought, he sharply responds.

"Can you do the same for me? I mean be honest and *REAL* too!" Devin demanded while arching his eyebrow to the highest point possible as he leaned towards me.

"I hear all the time how women want their man to look, act and behave, but when the mirror is turned on them, the reflection is quite ugly. If a woman plans to step with me, she has to be very sure of herself. I truly believe you are that woman."

"Damn, you're scaring me and lighten up will you?" I said, while breaking our whisper huddle at the table.

"You sound like you are talking about wrapping a business deal up."

We both break out laughing sounding like some crazed hyenas, which only draws more attention to the both of us as we stomped our feet and hit our hands upon the table. Normally, my mind feels trapped into the imagery of a certain scene, but this time I am not tripping off a damn thing. People seem to be so caught up with how someone looks, but later they're shocked to find out that the person or thing they admired is as weak as a half way dead lamb.

"Please, don't be afraid. I have done nothing to make you afraid of me. Just trust in life, love, and most of all- - - the Lord, and baby the rest will follow."

"Look, you have told me only what you think I should know. What is it that can make you ugly ass hell, or make me think second about being with a man like you? You know I really don't take a man too seriously for giving it up on the first meeting." I joked.

"I'm secure in myself to say that I can actually control myself quite well. I do not need a woman to make me feel like a man. That happened on the day I was created and that is what it will be until till the day I die, so having a special someone is only a nice thought...not a requirement."

"I feel ya."

"No, make sure that you really do Rae, because I don't ever want you to think that I actually have to have you in my life to live. I need you in my life to make everything pleasant, more tolerable, or shall I say...just plain mellow! Companionship with a special person can make life seem all the more bearable." Devin confessed in a prideful tone of voice.

"What about you, your family, your career?" I questioned as if I was a lead prosecutor.

"Okay here goes. Never married, both parents still ask me everyday "Have you found the one?" I am a venture capitalist, and I own several properties in and out of the states and I dabble in the real estate business from time to time. No sisters or brothers, and we have a pretty small and intimate family. No mental or medical history, but...I have a huge appetite to fed by you and only you." He said in one huge breath.

"Damn, could you leave a few spaces in between everything you say from now on so a sister can digest and comprehend that shit?"

"It's your world baby." He smiles while stroking his hand across my face.

"Well I am totally feeling you. I just want us to go slow and work on being good friends, and who knows how this will develop. I do want you to understand that I am In the process of strengthening my relationship with my daughter, so I am not interested in introducing you to her quite yet. She needs time to adjust to the changes as well." I said making sure; he understood that he would not get all of my time and attention. I just had to make it clear that Rachel is my number one priority.

"Baby, (he gently grabs my hand) I am here for you *and* her. I will wait on the both of you. I have plenty of work that will consume most of my time. Just promise to make time for me. I am a patient, not jealous lover."

"Thanks for understanding Devin."

"You're welcome, beautiful."

Okay, where do we go from here? I am feeling quite horny, but to my surprise, I will not be very disappointed if nothing happens between us tonight. Damn, what does this mean for me? Is the medicine really working, or the maybe it is the fact that I may be experiencing true love?

"Rae, by now you should know I love poetry. I just wanted to site this poem to you. This is how I've been thinking of you since our own *back stage concert*." He devilishly grins.

"A poet friend of mine by the name of 16 Bars put his magic on this and I just had to share this with you. He created this poem and emailed it to me. He said it would knock you off your feet and have us tussling in them sheets!"

"See, I knew that freak shit would appear before the night! I am so flattered that you love to cite poetry to me. We must go out to one of the hot spots here in the Lou, one night. My girl Mocha Latte is throwing down with her *"Got Lyrics"* poetry set!" *I'm trying not to wiggle with excitement in my seat while I attentively stare at Devin. This man has his shit together.*

"Okay, we must do that one night! You know I'm no def poet from the biggest jam on television, so bear with a brother."

Strawberries, Whip Cream and Chocolate

"YOUR DRIVING ME CRAZY
STRAWBERRY, WHIP CREAM AND CHOCOLATE TASTSY
I WANT TO TASTE YOUR JUICES ALL OVER MY LIPS
AND RUN MY FINGER TIPS ALL OVER YOUR BODY
I WANT YOU AND I NEED YOU
LIKE YESTERDAY
CAUSE I CAN'T WAIT UNTIL TOMORROW
TO BE WITH YOU
I YEARN FOR YOU WITH EACH SUN RISE
CAUSE I DREAM OF YOU EACH NIGHT
STRAWBERRY, WHIP CREAM AND CHOCOLATE DEIGHT
YOU GOT ME RUNNING RED LIGHTS
TO GET NEXT TO YOU
CAUSE IT'S MORE THAN SEX WITH YOU
WANT TO STICK TO YOU LIKE CRAZY GLUE
CAUSE I'M SO INTO YOU
I CAN TASTE YOU IN THE AIR I BREATHE
AND EACH THOUGHT THAT I THINK
IS FILLED WITH IMAGES OF YOU

My Souls Desire

I WANT TO DO TO YOU, WHAT THE NEXT MAN WON'T DO

OR CAN'T POSSIBLY DO, CAUSE HE CAN'T POSSIBLY DESIRE YOU

THE WAY I DO

I GET GOOSE BUMPS WHEN I THINK ABOUT YOUR TOUCH

AND DAMN NEAR GO INSANE WHEN I'M IN YOUR PRESENTS

YOU WHOA ME

A PURPLE RAIN UNDER A CHERRY'S MOON ON A MORRIS DAY

WANTING TO KISS IN EVERY WAY

EVER SO SOFTLY

AS GENTLY AS A BABY'S BEATHE, AGAINST A MOTHER'S FACE

YOU ARE ONE OF A KIND THAT CAN'T BE REPLACED

IF I HAD ONE WISH, IT WOULD BE YOU

MY STRAWBERRY WHIP CREAM CHOCOLATE JEWEL....

16 Bars said it best, “Life is what you make it, it's just that simple!”

“What do you think Rae?”

“Why you want me to serve you some dessert right now in this restaurant in front of all these people?” Our asses will be banned from this place and all their other out of state locations for life!”

We both released another round of thunderous laughs for the entire restaurant to hear. Damn he really knows how to make a sister feel. Passion...Umm, it sure is a sweet taste. Better than any dessert, that been placed upon my lips in a very long time.

We both gather our things to go and I noticed he left a one- hundred dollar bill on the table. We didn't order more than forty dollars worth of food. Damn, Devin is the true definition of style, and class. He is quite a man.

"Does our date end here Ms. Lewis?" He asks as he reaches for my door handle of my car.

I paused to look at what stands before me. I think Jennifer Hudson said it best when she won her Oscar. "See what God can do?" I love how that girl broke that crowd down with that statement! Yeah, she was not supposed to win, but she did! Now that is God's work at its best! I know I had nothing to do with how things were currently going with Devin. I knew it was no one but, the Lord. That thought alone made me want to sail like a yacht on the clear blue sea.

"I would love to spend the night with you, but I have to take a trip to Atlanta to spend time with my husband's family for the holidays. I am not looking forward to it, but my entire family will be there, and he is not quite ready to spill the beans about us being apart. My daughter is all ready down there with my sister. I feel between the both of them instigating shit and folks being nosy as usual, my family time will turn into fight time.

"Look, I'm not telling you how to handle your family business, but I hope I can give you a suggestion to think on."

"Speak."

"Rae, your husband and you both made mistakes. There needs to be some time as well as distance between the both of you. You seem to be a big girl, and with all that has been done unto you, whether it be inflicted by self, or at the hand of some one else, one thing stands out."

"That would be?"

"Your strength is not compromised by your tears, fears or anyone that has tried to hold you back from being who you are right now!"

"Call for your child and sister to come home. He needs to be a man and learn that it is time for him to face the monster that has finally come from the closet. That whole incident should be for him to explain. Not you."

"I..."

"You must wait your turn." Devin says while placing his finger upon my lips.

"Sorry."

"Clear your mind and spirit of that man. Learn that you will have to deal with him on an entirely different level. Respect him, forgive him and love him like a good friend as well as the father of your child. He will need that support, but right now, he has to understand that things must change, and he must be willing to accept it. Not showing up this year for the holidays will sting him like an angry mob of killer bees. I'm not telling you what to do; I'm just making a suggestion."

With those words, he reached inside of his suit jacket and gave me a large card.

It was his home address and home phone number, along with a poem written on it.

"Call me in case you decide to come over. I'll run your bath water and have the chocolate strawberry Fondue waiting." He said while flashing a devilish smile.

"Oh yeah, I will make sure your sister is compensated for gas and travelling fees if she decides to come back home at your request. I couldn't have it any other way." Devin said.

Standing back to his original six foot five frame, he extends his hand and I reach for it, then he gently kisses my hand.

"Thank you for a very fine evening, I hope you make it a beautiful and gloriously morning as well. Good night *Ms.* Lewis." Devin said while walking backwards toward his car, trying to catch ten eyeful images of my luscious frame as it hangs outside the door of my car.

"Gone head and spread them thighs!" he teases.

"Later." I teased back.

Who said starting over was hard?

~Chapter 15~

It's all about Rae!

I sat there motionless and feeling completely torn. Once again, my mirror pointed directly towards my face!

"Girl what are you going to do?" I asked myself while crazily staring into the mirror.

The more I thought about what Devin said, as I leaned against my plush and supple leather seats, everything started to make sense. The same actions equal the same results. I noticed that the New Year was just around the corner and hey, now is as good as anytime as the other; to make positive changes in ones own life.

"Denise?"

"Hey girl, you got some crime scene tape?" She angrily asks while trying to disguise her frustration.

"Girl what are you talking about?" I quizzed. I knew she was about to go nuts though. I can hear that crack in her voice all moms experience right before we break our feet off into our children's asses.

"I'm done playing mother hen, because **these kids have killed my ass**! Now, that is why I need the crime scene tape, because my ass is dead!" she finally blurted out, which ordered complete silence to fall in the background.

We both just started bugging up laughing.

"Denise, turn the rental car in and I'll fly yall home, tonight!"

"Rae, I knew I should have had that talk with you about being on them drugs and shit!"

"Heifer, I ain't on any damn drugs. I'll pay your way!" I announced.

"I'm packing now! I was just playing sis, you know how much yo lil sis loves ya. Glad you called; I was just sitting here trying to figure out how many kids I could stuff into the trunk on the car ride home!"

"Rae, what is going on?" she asks while shoving her ear against the phone. Does she really think that she can tell how I really feel as I share my drama?

"Lance made his choice and I will not be there to sugar coat and smooth shit out between him and his crazy ass family! I am so over with all that drama."

"Good! We will leave now and I will tell them it's an emergency back home."

"Okay, I'll call and talk to Lance myself. The next time I am in Atlanta, I will sit down and have a talk with his people. They need to be well informed from my point of view as well."

"Yeah, you know he gone leave some information out!"

"Like what Niecy?"

"Duh... like the gay part. You know folks always leave the truth out when they trying to come clean. Glad you came to your senses sis." Niecy says while she happily extends her congrats.

"Let's just say I had a very dear friend help me out." I confessed, thinking back to the conversation Devin and I had.

"Tell me bout him when I get home!" she whispered, while chastising the kids in the background.

Damn, this girl thinks she knows every thing.

"Rae?"

"What?"

"I do know everything."

CLICK!

I'll kick her ass when I get home. First, there is a call I need to make.

"Lance?"

"Hey Rae, how are you doing?"

"I'm well, thanks for asking. Look, I need to talk to you."

"Are you coming or not Rae?" he nervously asks, while lowering his voice. He must have been around the family.

"Don't piss me off! I'm trying to let you down the nice way; you really know how to push my buttons sometimes."

"Baby, please don't do this to me." Lance begs like the bum he is.

"Look, we both messed up, but what you have done is something I can't stand by your side on. I have nothing to do with your sexual orientation. This is a self-issue. Unfortunately it has destroyed many lives!"

"Stop it; you're being so ignorant right now." He cried. *Damn maybe those sissy tendencies were already there!*

"No, I'm not wrong. Do you know how many doors you opened that may never be closed? Life for everyone in this family is hard! Even some of our business associates will eventually find out about this!" Trying to show Lance that darkness has yet to fall upon us, will be a hard task to complete. Our drama must remain between us. Neither the media nor the courts need to be involved.

"I just need your support." Lance humbly confides.

"I can't help you Lance. There is really nothing to celebrate with you this Thanksgiving."

"You have nothing to be grateful for?"

The only things I am grateful for is being H.I.V. free, having a peace of mind, our daughter not being mentally torn up over our drama, and my sister. For some reason, I have peace in my life, Lance."

"Rae, Is this your measure of revenge?" Lance asks, while trying to not to allow his falsetto of anger to pierce my ears!

"Did you forget I had the pictures from the salon?" I snapped back on his ass. Wishing and hoping like a kid in the candy store for him to un-wrap my hard candied kick ass attitude!

"Go on Rae." Lance said in a more mellowed out tone of voice.

"No, it's my measure of starting a new life, without you. I apologize for marrying you and not being completely in love with you. I admit my reasons were for self-gratification only. After time passed I grew onto you, but I never fell in love with you. I mean be honest, how long did you really think our marriage was going to last?"

"I know, but baby I promise I didn't mean to turn out like this. I figured if I found the coldest woman that walked the earth in the summer season, have a child, and make lots of money, everything else would fall in place. This shit feels like I have been living a façade and no one will accept the real me once I appear. I'm almost afraid to ask, but I know some people will tell me I'm crazy and to move on as the old me, not some hot pants fagot!"

"Hey if they tell you that, then they don't love you! You can't continue to bottle your feelings up like medicine. You've lived a fucked up life long enough, its time you lived for you, Lance. I'm sure as hell doing it!" *Why am I talking him through his problem? I can't believe I am talking in a civil manner. I should be somewhere tearing shit up, defacing his image or his cars. What is up with me?*

"Does it have to happen this way?" he asks trying to see if there is room for negotiation.

"It doesn't, but it will. You try to explain to your parents now, and if you feel like I need to be there, then I will make the trip. I just feel this needs discussing with your parents. You never know, until you do it Lance." Shifting my thoughts back to Ray, I felt prompted to ask Lance another question.

"Are you and Ray official?" I asked in a nonchalant tone of voice.

"We chose to get counselling, and then we will take it from there. What I can say is outside of you, I will never have another relationship with a woman. I am not Bi-sexual. I am gay. I have fought that battle long enough."

"Please re-assure me that I did not turn you away from women."

"You know you didn't! You are the finest woman that has walked the earth."

"You know, I just want to walk away with a clear mind Lance."

"I understand."

"Please talk to Ray and explain to him that no story he gives, or scripture he cites will change the way I feel. I am on the path of self-discovery and I have forgiven him. I realize that I cannot move on with old *'soul wounds'*, still open to the elements. That could cause one major infection! He needs to focus on his self. Trying to make me understand his situation is not going to smooth things over any quicker."

"I will talk to him." Lance states in a very understanding and compassionate tone of voice. I guess the drama is over for now.

"Thanks Lance."

"Rae, are you still upset with me?"

"No, I just wish you could have talked to me a long time ago about this. Carrying luggage of that capacity around for all the years you have done is very damaging... mentally speaking. We both were wrong of doing this! Lance, you must know that I've fallen in love."

"Who is he?" Lance asks in a very surprising tone of voice. I can imagine how cockeyed and crazy he looks at this very moment.

"It's not a he...its Desirae Lewis!"

"Huh?"

"I fell back in love with the old Rae. The woman who not only did things for her self, but the woman who cared about who she was, what she stood for, as well as the way she treated her mind, body and soul. Self-love is the best love out there baby. I found out a few things about myself in therapy with my new doctor and now I have understanding, and a new peace about myself."

"I need to get me some of that." He responded.

"Just take time to explore you, and make the best efforts to let the real Lance Lewis flow like running water. Don't push a damn thing! Just let it flow. I promise you, the rewards will be sweeter than any guy you ever date!" *Damn, I could not let that one slide. Devin said a sister had some mad joking skills.*

"Rae!"

"What?" I responded as I smiled uncontrollably at the stab I just took at Lance.

"I'll love you always." He proclaimed in a very proud voice.

"Same here Lance. Oh yes, the attorney will be contacting you soon about the proceedings."

"Look at you, business as usual, huh?"

"You know it."

"Hey Rae, let's be civil about the divorce. I know our pre-nup states that if either party is caught cheating, the other party is awarded fifty-percent of the others assets. Can we agree to site another reason? I do not want this to get ugly."

"Lance, I will tell you this only one more time. I have forgiven you. You have enough on your hands. I'll do whatever to make sure our divorce ends quickly and civil."

"Do you still have those pictures?"

"Yes Lance. I promised not to use them. Just make sure you follow through with being civil and all will be well."

"Thank you Rae."

"Good night Lance."

Okay, I can finally start to feel more rocks roll off my back. I guess making peace is not always a bad thing. Yeah I had the proof that would allow me to half of what Lance owns, but my image is more important. I can imagine folks saying stupid shit like "She knew his ass was gay, or she married him for the money!" That's when I'm going to jail! People assume shit is easy to get in and easier to get out. Assuming shit ends when your knee deep in your own damn trouble.

My rear view mirror catches my eyes once again. This time I feel no shame as I stare directly back into the new me. I love the woman I am facing.

"Girl what are you staring at? You know damn well, that there is a beautiful, spirit- filled, and compassionate man awaiting your arrival."

I picked up the card that Devin gave to me and saw that he had written some other stuff within the card.

"Dear Rae,
I took the time to tell my friend Ausar, a poet friend of mines all about you. With that act, he created a poem all about you and me. I described to him where, when and how I want our relationship to grow. You are totally a breath of new life. You really excite me baby. I am looking forward to going…

Beyond
Sex

I'm gonna get straight to the point...
I want U!
I'm not trying to rush the sex,
because sex shouldn't be rushed.
It should be taken in slowly
with a sense of enjoyment.

Not empty & unfulfilled

like unemployment.

Because I'm ready to put in some work.

I'm talking about over a period of time,

which includes overtime!

And where I wanna take U...

is gonna take some time.

Do U wanna know where I wanna take U?

Beyond

Sex

I wanna take U into the unknown.

Into "deep" undiscovered erogenous zones.

I wanna go beyond those familiar sensations,

and create new temptations.

Because deep within U

there are new pleasures to find.

Pleasures that go beyond the physical...

I'm talkin' about your mind!

Because anybody can bump & grind,

but not everyone can pleasure your mind!

Causing U to have multiple mental orgasms,

sexual mind spasms.

Which not only makes your pussy wet,

but also causes your brain to sweat.

Beyond

Sex

I wanna take U deep into space.

I'm talkin' about a place

well into the universe.

A place GOD has yet to create.

A place when creation is made...

U & I would see it first!

Beyond

Sex

I wanna take U to your most extreme fantasy.

I want us to re-define ecstasy.

I want us to re-design sensuality.

I want us to re-fine sexuality.

Beyond

Sex

I wanna take U Beyond Sex

to where just the thought of me

causes U to lose your breath.

Hearing my voice

makes U cum all over yourself!

Just seeing me...
makes your clitoris erect!

I want it to be where
if someone were to ask U to give a description,
all U can do is show them your prescription.
Because it's an addiction
that only I can fix!
An addiction satisfied only with my dick!
A lick...
a lick so satisfying
that I've tattooed my tongue across your clit!

Beyond
Sex

I want U to experience total ecstasy
from head to toe.
I want it to be so
that when U cum, U cant' seem to stop.
And when U do...
U beg to cum some mo'!

Beyond
Sex.
Created by Ausar- Lord of the Perfect Black .Under the direction of yours truly,
Devin Anderson

I hope you have found this poem not only refreshing, but as an invitation to hear how my heart rapidly beats for your acceptance and devout love. You are truly, a divine work of art and a splendid child of God."

I couldn't hold back, half way through the letter I was playing with my pussy. Talk about some erotic shit!

"Dayum, he put it down!" I squealed as I held the card firmly atop of my breast as I gazed into the autumn skies.

I need to ride through the car wash with my top down I'm so hot and horny! My mind is *wet* with sweet images of this man. This thought alone...if it persists, will only send me into an instant relapse of searching for dick, like a full-time job.

With the turn of my key and a push on the accelerator, I was off for a tranquil evening with a man that magically placed himself into my life.

Can I get a damn towel please? He got me wet like a water park!

~Chapter 16~

One Last Dance

As I drove down the highway, my mind couldn't help but to wonder back to the times Ray and I spent together. Now I admit, I had feelings for this man, but at the same time, I felt like a fool. His love was very limited and conditional. I mean, if you claim that you want to be with someone; then that a person would find a way to make that special someone feel, hear, smell and hell, even taste your desires. That's what a good relationship means. Ray failed me in that area. He was so secretive. Hell, the only time I wanted to be with him more, was when he was *lifting* my insides! Why did I not see all the obvious signs? Maybe because I was too busy focusing on the wrong! You'll know when the right one comes along. You can feel his love through the phone line, the sound of his voice simply makes you lose control, like Silk. Hell, his scent drives you right to the front of his house. Oh, yes lest we not forget the taste of his lips when they first greet yours! Yeah…makes you want to go searching for that *new love* experience all over again! That *new love* will have you doing some crazy shit!

Was I the woman Ray was using to make sure that he was a full-blooded homosexual or the fact that he was using me to get at my husband for some shit that exploded between them? I don't sleep, eat or shit easy when my mind still pulsates with query.

"Ray, are you up?" I asked in a hurried voice, hoping his ass would be ready and willing to give me all the truth that stands.

"Hey, thanks for calling." He responds while clearing his throat to rid the grogginess.

"I don't plan on talking to you long, so please get on with your explanation."

"I love you. Lance is not who I want, it's you! I know this is such a hard thing to understand, but there is so much going on that you simply won't believe all of the mess I have to inform you of. Seeing the story is better than listening to it sometimes.

"What are you talking about Ray?"

"Please, life for me is not perfect and I admit I have made some mistakes, but please...take the time to listen to reason! Once you see what I have to show you, all thoughts of that husband of yours will be changed like a flat tire." Ray responds.

My heart suddenly slips out of my ass. I can't even think about some other shit that Lance could have done. I can't help but to bite on my lip while I consider a meeting with Ray.

"Have you and Lance been receiving counselling? He said the two of you were going to work it out."

"What? I have not contacted him since the night after you caught us. I really don't want to talk about this over the phone!"

"Spill it, or I'll hang up!" I threatened.

"Go ahead and be the biggest fool out there." Ray replied letting me know that whatever he had to spill, it would bring my ears to the point of a Doberman's Pinschers.

I paused then looked at my watch because I wanted to see Devin, but now some new shit has surfaced on the curb, that needs washing away!

"Rae, meet me in my office. That is where I have every piece of evidence you wish you had long time ago."

"I'll be there in a few. Don't bullshit me Raymond!"

Okay, should I call Devin and tell him that I will be there or should I surprise him? I am sticking to a limit of thirty minutes with Ray; from there I will be out and on my way to be with Devin. I want to wash everything dirty out of my life!

"Oh, were you following me Ray?" I asked out of surprise, as we arrived to the building at the same time.

"Baby, look..."

"Quit it with the baby stuff. Those days are so over." I snapped as I hurried up the steps.

"Those *'baby'* days may re-start once you see what I have to show you." Ray responds in a very confident tone of voice. This type of cockiness that Ray is spittin is the kind that guarantees him a good fuck! He knows I love a cocky, smart and brash son of a bitch! Ooh the nerve of this man right here! Confidence only spells out one way to me! It's simply S.E.X.Y! *Damn, should I be scared?*

"Ladies first, please." Ray said as he held the elevator door open. I hesitantly marched onto the elevator taking to my corner while Lance took to his corner. You would have thought that we were two pit bulls waiting for release, so we could shred one another apart.

"Rae, Lance set me up!" Ray blurted out.

"What are you talking about Raymond?"

"Well I was at a party that turned into more than what I had bargained for.

It started out as a net working event, but by the end, it became a social fiesta. You would have thought R-Kelly and Jay Z had stepped in on the scene."

"Huh, stop with the fucking dramatics!" I quizzed as I tried to keep my distance from the man that I once thought about making my number two hubby.

"A real fiesta broke out, because folks started to get buck wild. The smell of booty, pussy and Fritos, filled the air. The floors and walls sexily swayed with silhouettes of people grinding and sliding all over each other. "

"Get to the real shit, what are you trying to say?" I commanded the truth.

"Oh shit, what was that?" I screamed.

"Calm down, the elevators do this from time to time." He said while trying to open the control panel on the elevator wall.

"Hurry up and fix that shit, Ray!" I demanded while taking place closely against the wall, as I stood on the tips of my toes.

"I am trying Rae." He shouted back over his shoulder in a panicky type of voice.

From there my heart sank deeply into my stomach and I started to get queasy with nervousness. I can't help but to fall to the floor as the elevator drops even more.

"Be still Ray! Call the fire department and sit down. You're making the elevator drop!" I nervously whined.

"Okay, I'm sorry Rae." He pleaded while placing his hands on my shoulders to assure me all would be okay.

"Hi, this is Doctor Raymond Phillips. I am stuck in the elevator inside of my medical building, and I need assistance. The elevator keeps dropping, please send some one quick. There is also a woman stuck on here with me and she is sick with nervousness." He states in a very calm and concise tone of voice.

"Are they coming?" I questioned while I sat completely still, not even wanting to take a breath.

"Yes, they traced the address from my call. Be calm, help is on the way. He re-assured me.

"Okay, keep talking; finish telling me what you saw. I need to be entertained, distracted or something until the fire department gets here."

"Rae, I saw Lance on the couch getting straight out of stray jacket crazy with two dudes on the sofa."

"You saw what?" I cried.

"Yes, by two dudes. I remembered you showing me a picture of your family and my mind was totally thrown off, once I spotted him in all his glory."

"Hell to the double no!" I responded.

"He spotted me and he instantly charged towards me. I started to run, but what for. How did he know about you and me? I promised I never told anyone about you besides…"

"You told someone? Ray, please tell me who you spilled it to!"

"Mrs. Jones."

"Who is that?"

"You see her before you see me at my office."

"You're talking about Mrs. Jones, the receptionist?" I asked as I placed my hands over my mouth.

"Yeah, she's my mom. She re-married once after my father passed twelve years ago. "She's crazy in love with you Rae, so am I." Ray said as he grabbed my hand.

To my surprise, I didn't pull away.

"Next, Lance goes onto to say how he knows that I am the doctor that has been fucking his wife."

"I can't believe this shit!" I yelped out like a sick puppy.

"I told him to piss off and that he didn't know who he was fucking with, and then I pushed him to the side to leave."

"What did he do?"

"He grabbed my arm, and said that he knew it was me because the insurance claims for the services I rendered to you came to the house. He stated that you started acting funny a few months after you started seeing me. That is when his suspicions rose, along with thoughts about getting rid of you."

"That punk bitch!" I yelled.

"He must have put something together because I told him my therapists name was Archibald Reynolds. I never thought he would have looked into what I told him. I just threw him that name and I did on a couple occasions see that doctor, but..."

"What are you thinking Desirae?"

"I paid that doctor in cash. I never used my insurance. Damn, I figured the cost was so low, I did not mind paying out of pocket. Now, this only explains why he asked me who my doctor was not too long ago. I was sure I told him about Dr. Reynolds when I came to see you. I guess that was his way of confirming my lies. Wasn't that a bad move or what?" I still found myself holding on to Ray's hand while I was trying to piece this crazy ass puzzle together. What was making me hold onto his hand?

"Well wait, you won't believe this part. He then informs me that I was going to help him get rid of you. That is where the plan came to set you up, by exploiting, our affair occurred. He told me my reward was my image being saved and one million cold hard cash; along with none of the tapes being sent to my church members and work associates!"

Hell naw, Lance must have been planning this for a while. My mind erased the thoughts of not using those pictures against Ray in our divorce settlement. I need to dig some more. Ray is confusing me with all of the new shit he is talking.

"Can't I trust anybody at all?" I cried in disbelief while I cried into my hands.

"Ray, help me to make all this shit clear!" I angrily begged as I slammed my hand into the floor of the elevator.

"I was supposed to turn the tapes of you and me over on the night you caught us in New York, but I played his ass cold and told him, that I had forgotten the tapes in St. Louis. Sudden change of heart I guess."

"Yeah right, that good old religion kicked in Praise Jesus!" I rejoiced.

"Whatever!" Ray said as he waved me off.

"Okay, what about when you returned home?"

"I went on leave and my mother and brother ran my office. I decided to lay low until I could get in touch with you. That is when I was hoping to have the chance to better explain things."

"Then it happened."

"What is *it* Ray?" *I wish someone would hook me up to a defibrillator machine…I feel a heart attack on the way!*

"I guess he got pissed while I was lying low and he sent me and email."

"What was in the email Ray?"

"It was a video file. It was you and I doing our thang! It was the day of your confession. You do remember when you confessed your love for me, right. Well that tape was all he needed to end the marriage, make him richer and the chance to have sex with me."

"Huh?" I asked in that dumb and irritating tone like Lance used to do.

"Well he came to my office one day to tighten up our loose ends of the deal. I think that's when he planted the spy device."

"I'm still lost Ray!"

"I told Lance the day and time I planned on taping you and me. I think for added security, plus the fact that he never trusted me; he planted extra devices."

"When did he have time to do that?"

"I was in the john when he came into my office. He had to be waiting for about ten minutes."

My head hung all the way to the floor in pure embarrassment, and disbelief.

"Later that day he threatened (for the hundredth time) to use the tapes against me if I didn't fuck him! That email of us followed shortly, just to add extra-strength to his threat like Tylenol. He even threatened to mail them to my church members and the media. NOW, you see why I had to carry out with meeting him in you salon. I hated the thought, but I needed to *do him* in order to make my plan work!"

"Stop lying." I said while trying to read his face like a newspaper for the next story to slip from his lips.

"No, you need to wake up Rae! You can keep on fooling yourself by thinking the truth only flows on Sunday mornings, or save yourself right now Rae.

"He told me that he wanted to feel my warm juices inside of him! Lance told me if I did not do have sex with him; he would expose our sex tape to the media. I told you that already! I couldn't have your life and my life as well put on ***Front Street*** like that."

Now my mind is full of information. I am trying to add up all the tad bits from here and there like its tax season. I was trying to make sure I didn't miss something that would make me audit Ray's story all over again! It's hard trying to tell the truth from the lies right now. My ass is stuck and it does not look like I will be going anywhere for a while; damn a Snickers sure would come in handy! I got a huge hunger pain for the damn truth!

"Hey." Ray called out, as he lifted my chin upward in the cuff of his hand.

"What?" I asked while looking him in his eyes.

"I taped the smashing at your salon!" He proudly stated as he pounded his fist into his chest.

"You did what?" I asked in a school girlish type of voice as I sat up and regained my posture.

"My belt buckle had a camera in it. I open the zoom field wide and it taped everything that happened in the room. I made sure my face was out of view, so everything seen is from my waist on down. All you can see is Lila being tagged from the back by Lance, and Lance with an ass full dick! After the shit he pulled with threatening me I had to come up with a death defying get back!" I gasped. *Now we back on even playing ground. That bastard thought he had what he needed to bury me under the Arch, but now…his ass may be taking that spot. I just have to figure Ray out. He's still suspect to me.*

"That's why you went on a hideout when you got back huh?" I asked.

"Well, I wanted to get the tapes formatted and have a chance to speed you up on the real truth! Plus I needed time to get my mind right after that shit at the salon."

"Was Lila apart of the act Ray?"

"Nope, Lance wanted her in just to fuck her. He's too greedy, and he loves both worlds down under! From what I understood, he and Lila had been fucking for the last four months. He is certainly into cruising both markets." Ray laughed.

"Now even if he tries to use that tape against you, we can just show him our tape and guess what?"

"What?"

"His ass will back off, because we can simply state you did what you did out of the painful discovery of your husband being gay. We can even present the tape to him before he goes to his attorney if you'd like."

"Yeah, this way I can walk away with half his shit because he can't have his image destroyed! I know he would not take it far; he rides on his image too much! If it's one thing I know, Lance Lewis will not let his image be stained for no one or no thing! That is how he makes his money! I know with the evidence he think he has, he has already seen a lawyer. I'll call his lawyer and schedule a meeting. I bet you his ass will back all the way off!"

I cannot do a damn thing except thank the heavens; this did not turn out to be a total mess after all. I cannot let his ass off after finding all this shit out. The fact that Ray is looking to get even, shows his trueness and real love for me.

"I hope he goes blind, deaf, loses his scent, sensory skills, ***and*** his dick shrinks all in one fucking night!" I vented while pounding the elevator walls.

"Can't see no pussy, can't hear the pussy when it meows, no sniffing the pussy and damn sure no more fucking the pussy!" I exclaimed with pure vengeance while I held my fist high to the ceiling, as if I were fighting the powers that be.

We both just started bugging up! In all the time that has passed; I never imagined I would ever being able to share a laugh with Ray, after all that drama.

"I had on about three condoms! I tried to make sure I shredded his Ass apart! I know this sounds sick Rae, but looking at Lila's ass while thinking of you was my motivation! That Lance of yours is one sick puppy! He needs help!"

"No he needs to be exposed along with a good ***HOT WATER*** baptism!" I smarted off, while still giving Lance the good-eye! *I cannot believe the shit he just said. That is not a cool way for any dude to get back at another dude. I will have to log that shit into my memory bank. He is not out of the woods with me right now!*

"What about the story he gave me on how the two of you met?" I asked still wanting to be one hundred percent sure of the stuff he had just filled my head with.

"Like I said, he saw me at the sex fiesta! I never would have gone there if I knew that shit was going to break out like that."

"Wait, Ray, who called me from my salon then?" I suddenly had a flashback to the call that got my womanly instincts working mad over time. Hell, that phone call was the main reason why I flew to New York.

"I told him I had to go to the rest room to prepare myself mentally for what I was about to do with him. I left the room, ran to the front called your cell on your business phone, then hung up when you answered. After I made it back into the spa room, I told Lance to call and make sure that you were going to be in Miami, before we started our freak fest! That explains the second call after I initially called you. When I went back into the spa room, I delayed the event as much as possible by watching him and Lila do each other repeatedly. I told him I needed time to build my nerves up."

"You are too smart for your own good Ray."

"I knew that phone call would get you going. You're a smart woman Rae."

"Not too smart if I got played by Lance's dumb ass."

"I felt bad the whole time baby, but I could not let that dead booty ass husband of yours get away with making both of our lives a living hell." He replied while looking at his watch for the zillionth time.

"How have you been Ray, I mean really?" I asked while taking his hand into mine.

"Like I told you Rae, the last time we made love there was so much I wanted to tell you but it was so hard to do so. My judgment was blocked and all the choices I made really had me feeling like a total loser. Now do you understand the reason why I seemed so distant?"

"I do understand, however I have a question that needs the truth to follow. Are you gay? I mean fucking my husband to get back at him for what he tried to do to us is some wild, crazy, confusing and a little mentally disturbing shit! Please be honest with me." I asked Ray while giving him a comforting back rub. *I could tell Ray was about to break. This must have been a rough experience for him.*

"It was about saving our lives and our careers. I could not imagine being humiliated in front of the entire world on CNN, NBC, ABC and those other network media outlets. Damn could you imagine that shit? We know too many important people in and out of St. Louis!"

"Yeah, your right, but do you really love me?" I asked trying to regain some reassurance that Ray was not lying himself. I tried several times to get at Lance on his cell, but I could not get a signal on my damn cell phone!

"I'll show you baby." Ray said as he leaned over me.

Ray charged me with the most powerful kiss that laid me flat out on my back. My nipples pained so much because they were erect with desire as this man stretched out on top of me. My pussy was throbbing with excitement, while being pinched with pleasure. My juices rolled down my lips to the crack of my apple bottom. I could not resist the sweet taste of this man. Maybe this moment of pleasure will show how deep his love is.

"Ray I want to you so bad." I moaned while I opened his pants and took a handful of his full, swollen and passion-filled testicles. I gently massaged him the way he loved me to rub him, and then I slid my hand up his long, hard and erect dick.

"Ooh damn!" I screamed in ecstasy as the elevator dropped again. For some reason I was not scared with each jolt of the elevator but excited!

"Please, baby show Ray how much you miss him!" Ray begged while opening his shirt so he could place his chest against my breasts. There we were flesh on flesh, with our hearts beating in rhythm to the feeling of desire we had built between us. There was not a single person in the world that could stop this undeniable bitch called, *Destiny*!

I licked all up and down his body. Once I got to his mid- section I swallowed, sucked, and tickled every inch of his dick, until he lifted my petite but thick frame up onto him.

"Put it in baby." I begged while grinding upon him, and pressing my clit onto his rock, hoping he could feel how '*my girl*' was throbbing to the beat for his love to be deep inside of me.

"Naw, I want to taste you." He implored while staring at me with those big green melon eyes. *Is he fucking my brain or me? Damn!*

"Please do it, I hope you hungry baby!" I impatiently cried while wiggling with excitement, as I clapped my thighs together. While waiting quite anxiously for his lips to taste what real berry juice tasted like I felt my heart rate increasing.

"Dayum" I moaned, as I snapped my head from side to side. "This is what I needed." I yelled as my toes curled to a tight locking position. I just knew that whenever he cut me loose, I was going to get up looking like a fucking eagle by the feet. How long will I have to walk that shit out?

"I can give it all to you, Rae. Please give me a chance." Ray pleaded his case.

"Please baby, don't talk. Use your tongue for the job that faces you right now." I cried as I crazily rubbed my fingers through his curly hair while pushing his face, *back to the place*.

"Damn baby you taste so good."

He starts sucking and tickling my clit as if he just came off a five day fast! My eyes could not stay open. This man was licking me into a coma; I mean this shit was an anaesthetic or something. You would have thought a sista was being prepped for surgery the way he licked me clean. I could feel my thighs, arms and legs tingling and weakened by this other bitch, *Ecstasy*. I am about to lock his head clean up in my thighs! I can't help but to open and close my legs as if I was fanning a furious fire down below. The way he is working his tongue down there is unbelievable. It's like painting a freaking wall; the strokes of his tongue are like a paintbrush. Oh, yes his master of a piece tongue… is doing the damn thang!

"Fuking outstanding, Ray!" Was all I could moan as he continued to paint his picture of desire on my pussy!

As I lay out on the floor of the elevator, another jolt occurs. That jolt shifts Ray into another element. As he rises from beneath, I see my juices all over his face! I automatically think of Devin. The image of him coming up from eating me out at the concert sent creepy shivers up my spine.

Damn, I cannot do this to him…wait; I cannot do this to myself. Devin and I cannot get together tonight! What is my status? What is my problem? Can I be a woman with a high sex drive or could I suffer from a sexual disorder? Why in the fuck has this doctor not called me back with my test results? Okay, too many questions equal a yield sign. What should I do?

Lord, please send a sign. I need an answer.

"I got the condom on, you ready for me to enter baby?" Ray questioned, while he propped his muscular frame between my thighs. Before I could answer, I heard a voice, followed by a thunderous crack on the elevator door.

"Doctor Phillips, it's the fire department. Are you Okay?"

"We're fine, just scared and nervous as hell. Could you please hurry it up?" Ray responded. He seemed more pissed than relieved that the fire fighters were there to save us. *Thanks for the save Mr. Fireman! A sister can take a hint!*

We start moving at crack head speed to fix our clothes, our hair, and my makeup while I sprayed some my perfume to get rid of the lusty, sex smell that fermented in the elevator.

"Can we finish this tonight baby?" Ray desperately asked.

"Let's get to the office to examine the tapes and I want to see the video and start with a plan to get back at Lance. We can't let him get away with All the shit he has done."

"Okay Rae, I'm down with you. Trust me; fucking your husband was NOT the highlight of my year." Ray hissed as he hurried to zip up his trousers.

Damn I am so glad I did not call Devin to inform him of my visit. He doesn't deserve being stood up. Soon as the chance arises, I will call and inform him of my not going to be at Lance's side. Everything he said made sense.

"Grab my hand lady." The fire fighter instructed as he reached down into the elevator.

Once the fire fighter pulled us out, we all hugged one another. Ray and I probably thanked them a million times until they disappeared into the shadows of the hallway.

"Okay, you ready to see?" Ray asked.

"Press play." I commanded while holding my breath.

After we watched the tapes, Ray and I made a plan to rid Mr. Lance for the last time. We sat back, laughed, reminisced and apologized to one another about a thousand times.

Ray slid down to my end of the couch and looked me dead in my eyes. "Do you love me? Can you ever forgive me for what I've done?"

"Can you forgive me if I ask for time to think this whole thing out?" I replied before I could even be fair enough to think my answer out. That had to be the mental side of me, because the physical side would have opened wide and instructed all divers that the pool is officially open.

"I can do whatever you need and want me to do Rae." Ray replied. Devin was on my mind tough. I still had some self- issues I was dealing with and I never found out the results to my lab tests, so once again...what is a woman to do? Is this my pussy talking, or is this the real Rae? Fuck, there's so much to understand while yet I have two men that really care about and want to be with me. I knew what I needed to do.

By the look in Ray's eyes, he knew what was coming next. He slowly backed away from me.

"Ray, this is not about us, it's all about me. I need my space and I need my time alone right now. Tonight has been too much to swallow. I have to make sure that the next man I'm going to be with is the one I want in my life, desire and truly love with all my heart. My desires right now, uncontrolled, or un-treated will only lead me to hell. No one is worth losing my soul for."

"You don't love me?" he asks.

"I love you very much. I just need some me time." I slowly explained.

"Ray, sometimes the wrong people get together for the right reasons."

"What, you just confused me Rae."

"Well, although two people may truly love one another and share some things in common they may not really be right for one another. A couple has to complement each other one hundred percent, and they both have to be on the same page in life. This is the reason why people grow apart. Right now, we have too many issues that need our attention. We can't possibly focus on one another with all the other drama we have to kill. This shit gone take some work!

"Well, I love you baby and no matter what you do…I'll be here for you. Shall we dance my lady?" he asks as he stretches his hand out.

I grabbed his hand and with a click of the remote, we were dancing until the suns rising to the sweet sounds of Will Downing. *At least Ray knows how to calm a sister down.*

Suddenly those damn shivers come over my body and I can feel my moisture level rising. I pull Ray closer, and he responds by pressing his semi hard dick right onto my *regions*.

"Rae, what is wrong with you girl, grab your shit and run! Love ***yourself*** first."

"Momma, is that you?" I asked, while searching frantically to see if a vision or ghostly like image of momma was in the suite.

"Rae, are you okay? Ray asks while he examines me.

"I think you have been up to long, you need some rest." Ray suggests as he continues to examine on.

"I need to leave. I think my mind is playing tricks on me."

"Okay, we'll walk down the steps together. It is going to be okay. Rae, please don't go into hiding on me."

"I won't. I promise you Ray."

We left the office hand in hand laughing and chatting like good friends.

The sun slapped the hell out of us as we left the building; but we both welcomed the new day with beaming smiles as we kissed each other good-bye.

While driving home I passed by the cemetery where my moms and pops were resting and yelled out a sweet thank you, to the man that planted the seed of life and the woman that birthed that seed.

"Thanks momma. I really needed that. You saved me. I'll always love you. Love you too daddy!"

"Anytime for you baby, you know momma always got your back." A sweet, gentle, and familiar voice whispered back.

I wasn't scared to hear her voice the second time around. Instead, I invited momma to talk to me. I didn't get a response but I am sure that she will come whenever I need her.

I really didn't know what to do in regards to Devin and Ray. My *drive* still urges me to go on a ride with Devin. However, I can't get that man out of my mind. We can be miles apart, and the thoughts of the way he had a sister bent over that speaker on the night of the concert makes me wanna holla! Its two things, okay three things good dick will make you do. One, fall straight to sleep in fetal position with ya thumb in ya mouth. Two, go straight stir jacket crazy and become a stalker! Three, make you get straight up, clean the house, cook a Sunday soul feast, braid ***all*** your *chilren's* hair, while humming *"Whatever"* by Miss '*Jill Jazzn Thangs Up*' Scott!" Ooh damn...sister needs a bottle of control right now!

I do feel one more trip to Devin's house is in order. I want to be able to tell him face to dick... I mean face to face that I want to take things slow while I address my mental health. Sister must have her mind right to deal with this daily episode we call life! Plus, I still need my space. Jumping from one relationship to the next is just unhealthy. That leaves too much room for bad judgment and error, in the new relationship. Although, who the fuck gone give me a good shovin with a side of lovin? I guess I had better go to the *toy store* soon!

I'm letting *(right after I see Devin)* go, and allowing the Lord to do what *he* does best! I know I should leave vengeance to the Lord; but the temptation to put the plan Ray and I made into motion for Mr. Hot Pants Lance, sits right on my lap. I can guarantee he will not be seeing any *golden bridges* any time soon. Part of me wants to let victory have its dance on court day, and the other part. Rip his fucking heart part! The Lord better work on me by sunrise, because this plan has already gotten the green light!

I decided to check my voicemails on the phone and to my surprise, the answer I was looking for was only one message away.

"Rae, its Dr. Daniels. Your test results came back and your blood levels are out of control. Truthfully, I think you have been suffering from severe depression. I am ***not*** ruling out the hypersexual diagnosis, but some other issues are on the horizon. Please call me. Some things you opened up about in regards to your past may be apart of what you are currently going through. Please do not ignore what I am saying. Feel free to call me anytime. My phone is always on. Burying something that is not dead will arise eventually, Rae."

"What the fuck!" All I want to do is cry right now. I am trying not to focus on the past, but at this point, I feel nothing is going to go away. Did I really want to deal with this right now? I had my health, my daughter, my freedom and one million...two million, oh hell I'm losing count! The money I get from the divorce will be enough to live off for the rest of my life. Am I ready to face my past in the midst of all that is going on? Can I simply move on from here? Can't the past, remain the past?

The drive home seemed to last three sunrises. Nothing was on my mind except a hot bath, and a nice glass of wine. I hope that by the third song on Jill Scott's, *'Collaborations'* CD, a sista will be deep into the land of sleep! I can't wait to sleep this day away!

After my relaxing bath, a good rub down and a quick prayer for guidance and strength, my door bell rings.

"Ooh no!" I cried backing up about fifty feet from the door. Why is Devin here?

"GIVE ME A FEW!" I yelled hoping it would give him a hint that he is really intruding on me. Damn, why is this happening? See, just as soon as you try to do right, the devil gets the green light to bring you down!

I opened the door and this was not on the devil, for what I saw standing before me was nothing but the good work of the Lord!

"Can I come in?" Devin asks while shaking the light drizzle off his raincoat. *Lord please tell me he ain't naked under his raincoat.*

"Yeah, come on in. What made you come by so sudden and umm…unannounced?" I quizzed while taking note that he was butt baby naked under his trench!

"You never called me back. I feared you leaving and I really had to see for myself if you were home or not. I don't think you understand how I feel about you Rae." Devin stated as he dropped his wet raincoat onto my foyer floor.

Backing up as if he is the strangest man in the world, my mind starts to wonder. This brother is scaring me. I really do not know much about him, but on the other hand, his strength, his vibe, his…yeah; his dick is enough to make me wanna find out more about him.

Reaching out with my hands as if I am begging for mercy for him not to have a reason to dick me down, I begin to state my reason for not visiting. "Devin, I'm cool, I just need some time to think for me, Rachel and my family. I have my businesses to run and hey- I need to recover. Damn, the lawyer has not even received the papers yet. Please back off.

"Nope, but you can back up on this dick!" he states as his hand gently strokes his dick.

"Oh hell, now you got jokes!"

Next thing I knew we were embracing one another and the kissing was so hot to where I felt a melt down on the way. The walls started to spin; my petite frame began to feel as if it were floating throughout space; while my mind danced around the sweet thoughts of Devin, tapping scores of erotic beats into my backside. Something tells me this extravaganza between Devin and I will last until the suns fall and well into the moons rising.

"Open up and let me inside. I want to feel your rain. Warm me up and give in to me baby." Devin encouraged me as he whipped his tongue around my firm nipples. My insides...I refused to let them run out a fluid of emptiness. My insides alerted me that a shower of love was on the way down. I trembled with anticipation, while my knees collapsed from weakness. This man is filling me up with so much passion, desire and newness. Is there anything wrong with feeling good?

"Show me why I need to keep you in my life Mr. Mystery Man! I feel you, but show me. You know you got the best pussy in the world, so toss it into the sky, so you can show the rest of the world what real sunshine looks like! Make me feel golden baby!"

The room started to spin again. My eyes opened and closed so many times that I felt as if I was trying to fight off the sleep fairy. One minute I was there the next I was out of it. Damn, what is it about this man than makes me lose control like Silk?

Night came upon us and reality broke the silence.

"Devin, I need for you to leave."

"Excuse me? What seems to be the problem, Rae?" Baby, just lay back and relax. You can't work it all out on your own. Let time work the matters in your life out."

"Time is good, but I prefer to spend it alone. You know right now, I have too many issues on the table to deal with. I can't give myself to you one hundred percent." I stated while getting up to use the bathroom. *I do not know why brothers cut up the way they do, after they have been told, NO!*

"Look Rae, apparently there are more things that you have not confided in me about, so you're right. You do need to be alone. Call me when you are ready. My work will keep me busy until then."

I watched Devin for any evidence to see if he was pissed. Surprisingly he wasn't. *Well that is what the fuck he appeared to be!* He walked his fine self on over and kissed me on the forehead. The kiss was not anything like Ray's kiss though. Ray kisses me as if love will be there no matter what. Devin's kiss was hard and forced. Thank God, for this alert button called...INTUITION! His ass *IS* mad and I do not give a hot damn with a side of hot fries!

"I'll constantly be thinking of you. Call me, Rae. I'll be waiting on the both of you." He stated as he pointed to my favorite picture of Rachel and me on my nightstand. I watched him walk away until he disappeared. I knew he was gone when I heard the door shut. I gotta let that man go, something ain't right about him.

I turned over and looked high up into my vaulted ceiling. The Angels I had the interior decorator paint on the ceiling danced and smiled down on me. I smiled back, because I knew after tonight, tomorrows sunrise will certainly be full of changes. The only question...how much of it will be on good old Rae's behalf and how much of it will be on the good Lord?

Sunrise came and I was ready to handle business. As I prepared to leave for a meeting with the attorney, I noticed another one of Devin's *love* notes on my foyer table.

"Oh Lord, this man and this poetry is going to kill me!" I cried out as I opened the letter.

"Dear Rae,

Without me in your life, you will feel that you have made the worst choice ever! Be smart and make the right choice.

Love, (I hope)
Devin"

Okay, my mind starts to jog and before I knew it, my forehead was sweating from the thoughts that raced through my mind. I know damn well that there is only one person who I told that same thing to and I know who HE is!

"Ray, wake up! What was the last thing I told you before you told your mother to leave for the day, when I was in your office on my last visit?"

"Rae, what the hell is going on? Why are you asking me about that?

"Answer me dammit!" I crazily demanded.

"You said something like I would feel as if I made the worst choice ever if I didn't decide to be with you. Baby, what is this call regarding? Get some rest Rae and let it go! You can't make everything better on your own. I will be here if you need me, Okay. Don't worry we will fix Lance, Rae.

"I'll be fine. Don't worry Raymond. I will keep in touch, before I tend to any legal issues; Rachel and I are going on a trip. I'll cal you when I get back."

"Be safe and enjoy yourself. You deserve it." Ray sweetly announced while yawning in my ear.

Okay, funny how both Ray and Devin seem to say the same damn things, that only I have told them or things that they seem to say to me all the time. There's a connection and I don't know where it going, but something tells me I may need Lance down the road. I'm applying the brakes to my plan on seeking revenge from Mr. Lance. I'm going to go on the down low myself and think of a master plan to rid ALL these jokers out of my life for good! Everyone telling me, *"not to worry and don't try to fix shit,"* well I am going to fix thangs all right. I do not know what in the hell is going on, but if the Lord brought me to it; he will get me through it! Lord, show me the way.

Like I have said before; with every sunrise, change gone come. Let us see what change brings us today!

Desirae Lewis is about to have all her...Desires Fulfilled.

One Last Word from Rae

My soul desires so much, but if I had to lay out my top four, they would be passion, peace, courage and plenty of self-love. I have my issues but as I said earlier, I expect no one to help me, but self and my sweet **JESUS!** Walking away from everything and allowing God to handle it all would be the sensible thing to do. However, what about when it is your turn? Can you let go and let God?

You see, when passion is present your willingness to do anything is unstoppable. You will find yourself loving what you do morning, noon and night. No one can make you hate what you do, because you love it.

Peace? Yes, peace in our minds, hearts and spirits equals rest in ones life. It means that you are well with all that which resides in this universe. If you have something/someone in your life that is full of hell, rage, frustration or violence. Remove it! Two negatives cannot start a damn thang positive!!!

Courage is what you need to stand against anything or anyone. Obstacles are ready for placement on the road before you even decide to turn onto it. Be prepared at all times and keep a trunk full of courage. You never know when you may need it.

Self-love really needs no explanation, but I am going to give it to you any way! When you love you, the feelings show one hundred percent.

People around you take notice that not only do you look good, but also your spirit shines bright, full of joy, rich and kind.

People love to be around great spirited people. Do you need examples? Okay, here are a few.

Tyler Perry, Oprah, Maya Angelou, Jill Scott and so many other outstanding individuals. If you neglect yourself, then whom do you expect to care for you. Only you can do you at one hundred percent. You know your goals, desires, dreams and everything you want to happen. Never put yourself on the back burner for anyone else.

I want to leave you with a poem. Take the time to read it, meditate upon it, and pray that it inspires you to fulfil your desires of living a happy, ***passion*** filled life. So many people live unfulfilled lives. Stop allowing your chores, duties, careers, rule your life. STOP IT! Trust me, if you died today, life will continue to moves along! Take the time to live life for you. For all my married sisters and brothers, take the time to find one another again. Take time to embrace, appreciate, and show admiration and love for one another! Remember that first kiss, that first touch and oh yes…that first fuck! Love hard and play dirty…in the dark, or under a pile of covers. Then let it roll like the good times baby.

Do not allow work, children and other tasks to pull you away from the one you love. You can still be excellent parents, but the kids do not run a damn thing and they do not deserve anything but a place to eat, sleep, shit, love, along with some clothing and peace in their lives. The rest is just extra! At least that is what my momma told me! If you continue to live life and not seem to care about yourself or those that surround you, just leave the door open for the new love interest to walk in and take your spouse. They will thank you in the morning, trust me! Do not worry about good old Rae, I'll continue to live on and pray that all my *souls' desires* are highly fulfilled in Gods good timing. No desire…no matter how much it heats every part of your body is worth going to hell for. Only God can make it happen, just as long as you acknowledge him in all of your ways, peace will be with you always. I gotta go, First Lady looking for me! I can't go back on my promises.

My Souls Desire

THIGHS CLAPPING YOUR NAME LIKE DESTINYS CHILD SANGS
IS ENOUGH TO RIP YOUR JEANS RIGHT OFF YOUR ASS!
THE TENDERNESS OF MY BREAST ALL MELTED IN YOUR MOUTH
ISN'T ENOUGH SO YOU SLIDE DOWN…
MORE TOWARDS THE SOUTH

AS I TRY TO PUSH YOUR FACE TO THE PLACE
YOU FEEL IT'S TIME TO MAKE THAT CALL----TALKING
"HEY YO, IT'S DADDY AND I AIN'T EVER COMING HOME!"
KNOWING DAMN WELL THIS AIN'T HARLEM -AND NO-
IT DOES NOT HAVE TO BE THE NIGHT TIME
IN ORDER FOR IT TO BE THE RIGHT TIME!

WHAT'S WRONG? DON'T GET MAD NOW AS I PULL YOUR CARD LIKE I PULL YOUR MAN
WHOS ALL HARD AND READY TO GET TO THE POINT!
AS I TAKE A HIT OF IT, I THINK-----YO- HIS SHIT IS THE JOINT!

YOU STILL SCARED? DON'T BE!

LAY BACK

CLOSE YOUR EYES

NOW PREPARE TO FEEL WHAT ITS LIKE

TO HAVE SUDDEN DARKNESS AND WETNESS OCCUR

ALL IN ONE NIGHT

OH YEAH, DID I MENTION THERE WASN'T A FUCKING STORM

CLOUD IN SITE!

AS YOU TUNNEL YOUR LOVE *THROUGH MY* LOVE

U FEEL THAT THE FITTING OF ME ON YOU--- JUST RIGHT!

U SEE, MY DESIRES FOR SOME REASON CANNOT BE

FULFILLED.

THIS GUYS TRIED, THAT GUYS TRIED, BUT STILL THERES NO

PLEASN

I PRAY NIGHTLY, TRYING TO REASON WITH THIS SPIRIT OF

LUST HOPING IT WOULD BE STILL

ONLY I AWAKEN TO FIND THAT MY WILL HAS BEEN KILLED.

ALL BY THE PASSIONLESS LIFE I LIVE.

U SEE, WITH PASSION THINGS CAN GROW

THE DESIRE TO BE REAL, HONEST AND HAPPY WITH SELF

My Souls Desire

IS SOMETHING NO MAN CAN GIVE

EVEN IF WEALTH HAS BEEN ATTACHED,
MY SOUL WILL FEEL THAT YOUR MONEY IS NO MATCH!

THEREFORE, MY SOUL WILL DESIRE MANY
UNTIL TRUE PASSION SCRACTHES ME

ONLY THEN WILL MY SOUL BE FREE!

Desirae

Let's talk about it!

1) Do you think Desirae had a high sex drive or a sexual disorder? Would you be able to distinguish between the two?
2) Which man do you think is right for Desirae, Ray or Devin?
3) Do you think Desirae handled the salon drama amongst the females Okay?
4) Do you think Desirae and Ray should carry out with their revenge plan against Lance?
5) Do you feel Desirae lacked self-esteem?
6) Do you believe Ray was truthful with Desirae? Could he still be involved with Lance? How being so?
7) Was Desirae a good mother?
8) Do you think Desirae really loved herself?
9) Do you think Desirae should have kept her composure and walked off, or was it okay for her to go nuts in the spa on Lance, Ray and Lila?
10) Do you feel that lack of self -love is a person's worst enemy?
11) Was it possible for Desirae to be in love with two men at the same time? Have you ever been in love with two or more people? How did you get to that point?
12) Do you think Devin is an awful nightmare waiting to come from underneath the covers?
13) Place your head on Desirae's shoulders. What would you have done differently?
14) Do you think Desirae acted out because her relationship with Lance lacked love and passion? Do you feel Desirae was simply a woman out of control?

15) How did you feel about the poems in the book? Did the poems make you examine your sexuality? What is your outlook on marriage, relationships and romance?

16) What did you think about Devin's note to Desirae? Do you think Devin is dangerous and up to no good?

17) What are your ideas for the sequel? What can you imagine happening?

18) Why do you think Desirae never really talked about her past? What do you think she is suppressing?

Email your answers to soulsdesire@londab.com

About the Author

Londa B.

Londa B. *(Raised as Yulonda M. Brown)* is a native of St. Louis, Missouri. She resides with her husband of ten years Chad, and her children Chanda, Marcia, and Chad Jr. She is also the proud owner of an English Mastiff named Sir Oliver. In her spare time, Londa B. loves mentoring the young women of today encouraging them to become strong minded, confident, and successful women of the future. She also involves herself in monthly meetings with women that focus on the power of self-love, self-preservation, and sisterhood within the community.

▒ Travelling and giving motivational/inspirational speeches is also one of many tasks on her agenda. She is also an active member of, Midwest Page Turners Book/Review Club. Women from all lifestyles discuss the "Book of the Month," and issues that evolve around SELF-LOVE, SELF-RESPECT, and SELF-PRESERVATION. Most of the members are also authors, poets and speakers that also volunteer their time to the St. Louis Community." In her spare time, she is a content producer for, Associated Content. An online site where authors publish their media stories for exclusive and non-exclusive publishing. Londa B. is also the chief editor, and publisher of Purposeful Literary Publications. In this literary newsletter, Londa B. highlights authors, poets, writers, and other artist. This publication is in circulation throughout the Midwest. To request a copy email her staff at: purposefullit@yahoo.com

▒ Londa B's dream is to open an outreach/resource center for young women that offer a variety of classes and seminars. The seminars would offer advice on becoming independent, completing high school and obtaining a college degree, financial advice/help, and an array of other services to help young women blossom into productive women of the future. Re-inventing the love of "sister- hood" is a very heartfelt dream of Londa B's. Currently, she is living her dream as the owner of Aminia Books and Publishing.

▒ Check Londa B. out at: http://www.londab.com or email her at: .talk2me@londabcom OR www.myspace.com/londababy

▒ Also, check out the authors other release: *"Who's Loving Me"* released in Nov 2006 through Author House, which is for sale through all online bookstore retailers.

Ausar
Lord of the Perfect Black

Author of: "Beyond Sex" & "You"

The Worls's awakening is not by a hot cup of coffee, but by the sensual, soul stirring, nerve vibrating, mind blowing and breath taking poems of Ausar. A floetic poet with a great stage presence was introduced to his new love by ending an old love. The first young woman he ever gave his heart to, broke his heart by leaving him for another guy with money. With pen in hand, Ausar took his feelings to the paper. In an instant, his poetic flow filled the pages to the entire notebooks end. It was there that Ausar had a newfound love...POETRY!

On the spoken word tip, it was back in 1998 when Ausar saw a spoken word performance. The "word bug" bit him so deeply that it left a very powerful, spirit filling serum that would allow this 'Lord of the Perfect Black' to spit out poems that would impact the world. Ausar's poetry includes topics that range from love, romance, erotica, social consciousness, religion and spirituality, black consciousness, and family issues.

Ausar first entered the world of spoken word in 1998 in the city of St. Louis where a bite by the "spoken word bug" occurred. His performances include Legacy, The Haraambe Institute, Raw Sugar, The Afrikan Village, and Lyrics of the Lou, all in the city of St. Louis where many received him with open arms! Ausar moved to the city of Atlanta in the year 2000 where he got heavily involved on the spoken word set. He performed at various venues around the Atlanta Metro area for a couple of years before producing & hosting his own spoken word show at the C'est Bon Cajun Restaurant Bar & Grill in Lithonia, GA. Some of Atlanta's top spoken word artist came to perform at his show. Those who came thru to spit include Def Poetry artist Abyss, Dana Gilmore, Jon Goode, and Tommy Bottoms. Last but not least, Cocktails, Freedom Speaks, and Khari B. (Chicago).

Ausar has just released his first book of poetry entitled, "Oral Elixir". The spoken word CD will soon follow. This book covers a wide range of subjects, so there is something of value in it for everyone. His work is an erotic wonder. Which inspires individuals to take a journey into 'self' and explore many avenues. Go ahead and check this brother out! You will not be disappointed.

To contact Ausar about performances, and book signings you can e-mail him at imausar@go.com, www.theperfectblack.com or at www.myspace.com/talk2ausar.

XVI BARS:

"Life is what you make it, it's that simple!"

www.myspace.com/stl16bars

XVI BARS, born Rundell Irvin has been writing poetry for eighteen years. He is a spoken word artist who has done shows throughout the Midwest.

Performance locations are; South East Missouri State University, Lincoln University, the Jazz Loft, Raw Sugar, Got Lyrics, Legacy Books and Cafe`.

XVI's graced the stage with such acts as Nelly, Saul Williams just to name a few. XVI's stories are from the heart. His stories paint pictures about things that he has been through, going through or things that he has seen in his lifetime.

Holding strong to what he believes, "It's not how much you write, but what you write that makes a difference."

Printed in the United States
200351BV00002B/526-537/A

9 780979 915475